MANDIE
AND THE
ABANDONED
MINE

Mandie Mysteries

1. *Mandie and the Secret Tunnel*
2. *Mandie and the Cherokee Legend*
3. *Mandie and the Ghost Bandits*
4. *Mandie and the Forbidden Attic*
5. *Mandie and the Trunk's Secret*
6. *Mandie and the Medicine Man*
7. *Mandie and the Charleston Phantom*
8. *Mandie and the Abandoned Mine*
9. *Mandie and the Hidden Treasure*
10. *Mandie and the Mysterious Bells*
11. *Mandie and the Holiday Surprise*
12. *Mandie and the Washington Nightmare*
13. *Mandie and the Midnight Journey*
14. *Mandie and the Shipboard Mystery*
15. *Mandie and the Foreign Spies*
16. *Mandie and the Silent Catacombs*
17. *Mandie and the Singing Chalet*
18. *Mandie and the Jumping Juniper*
19. *Mandie and the Mysterious Fisherman*
20. *Mandie and the Windmill's Message*
21. *Mandie and the Fiery Rescue*

———

Mandie's Cookbook

MANDIE
AND THE
ABANDONED
MINE

Lois Gladys Leppard

BETHANY HOUSE PUBLISHERS
MINNEAPOLIS, MINNESOTA 55438

Mandie and the Abandoned Mine

Lois Gladys Leppard

Library of Congress Catalog Card Number 87–70883

ISBN 0-87123-932-9

Published by Bethany House Publishers
A Division of Bethany Fellowship, Inc.
6820 Auto Club Road, Minneapolis, Minnesota 55438

Printed in the United States of America

With love,
to my granddaughter,

Natalie Rae Leppard,

that precious blue-eyed,
blonde-haired darling,
not yet old enough
to read about Mandie,
but old enough to love books.

"Children, obey your parents in the Lord: for this is right. Honour thy father and mother; which is the first commandment with promise" (Ephesians 6:1–2).

About the Author

LOIS GLADYS LEPPARD has been a Federal Civil Service employee in various countries around the world. She makes her home in Greenville, South Carolina.

The stories of her own mother's childhood are the basis for many of the incidents incorporated in this series.

Mandie Mysteries

1. *Mandie and the Secret Tunnel*
2. *Mandie and the Cherokee Legend*
3. *Mandie and the Ghost Bandits*
4. *Mandie and the Forbidden Attic*
5. *Mandie and the Trunk's Secret*
6. *Mandie and the Medicine Man*
7. *Mandie and the Charleston Phantom*
8. *Mandie and the Abandoned Mine*
9. *Mandie and the Hidden Treasure*
10. *Mandie and the Mysterious Bells*
11. *Mandie and the Holiday Surprise*
12. *Mandie and the Washington Nightmare*
13. *Mandie and the Midnight Journey*
14. *Mandie and the Shipboard Mystery*
15. *Mandie and the Foreign Spies*
16. *Mandie and the Silent Catacombs*
17. *Mandie and the Singing Chalet*
18. *Mandie and the Jumping Juniper*
19. *Mandie and the Mysterious Fisherman*

Mandie's Cookbook

CONTENTS

1. A Sad, Bad Mine 9
2. The Store-bought Dress 21
3. Waiting 33
4. Another Secret Tunnel 45
5. The Woman with the Dress 58
6. Mandie and Joe in Trouble 69
7. The Search Begins 84
8. Adrift in the River 95
9. Forgiveness 105
10. Explanations 117
11. A Mysterious Find 132
12. The Secret of the Mine 147

MANDIE'S TRAVELS

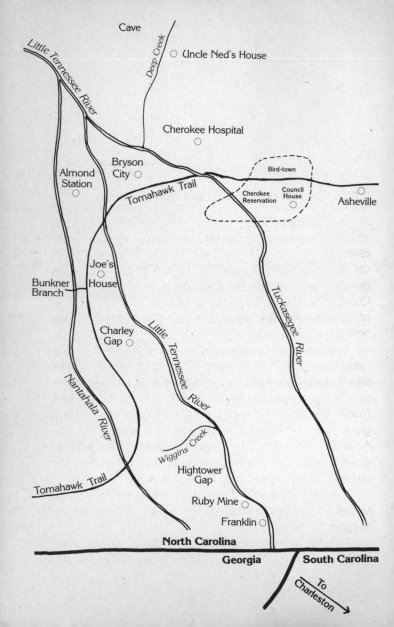

Chapter 1 / A Sad, Bad Mine

"Is this what a ruby mine looks like?" Mandie Shaw asked her Uncle John as she stared in surprise. All she could see was what looked like a plank floor covering the ground, going down the hill out of sight toward Rose Creek, a branch of the Little Tennessee River. The sound of voices and hammering came from beneath the boards.

Uncle John dismounted and offered his hand to help twelve-year-old Mandie down from her pony. Her white kitten, Snowball, squirmed in her arms as she slid down.

"Well, this is not exactly a typical mine for western North Carolina," he explained. "Most ruby mines don't go underneath the ground like this one. You see, Amanda, the dirt has to be dug away until you reach the gravel. Instead of digging a tunnel, you just scrape the dirt off the top. The rubies are in the gravel."

Mandie's long-time friend Joe stood nearby with his father, Dr. Woodard, listening. "Then why is this one underground?" Joe asked.

"Probably because this mine is about nineteen feet deep, and the depth of the dirt was so great that it made a huge crater when they dug it away. When they closed the mine years ago, they must have had to cover it with boards to keep people and animals from falling in," Uncle John explained.

"Why was it closed, John?" Dr. Woodard asked. "Was it mined dry?"

"No, I don't think so. I don't remember ever seeing it worked. I was small when my father closed it. It must have been nearly fifty years ago, around 1850. I remember hearing that there had been some special reason for closing it, but I don't remember what. In fact, I was forbidden to go near it when I was a child," Uncle John told them.

"How do we get under there to look for rubies?" Mandie asked, flipping her long blonde braid behind her back.

"As soon as the workmen shore up the timbers, we'll be able to go down inside," her uncle replied.

"But how? I don't see any entrance," Mandie said, looking around.

Uncle John pointed to an opening in the boards. "There are steps going down over there. The opening was covered over with the planks, so the workmen had to hunt for it. We were surprised to find it in fairly good shape, considering how many years it has been closed."

"Is this where our family got all its money?" Mandie asked, holding Snowball tighter as he tried again to get down.

"Part of it," Uncle John replied. "My grandfather, who was your great-grandfather, was in on the gold rush when gold was discovered here in our state at Concord in 1799. Most people don't know that the first gold discovered in the United States was found there. There was so much of it that the government had to open a mint in Charlotte about 1837 to take care of it."

"You mean the original gold rush was here in North Carolina and not in California?" Joe asked.

"Yes, it was some fifty years before the California discovery. Not only that, but gold was also found on Cherokee land before the rush to California. That was the main reason the white people moved the Indians out," John reminded him.

"Gold can do terrible things to people," Dr. Woodard remarked.

"Why does everybody have to be so money crazy?" Mandie sighed. "Was my great-grandfather money crazy?"

"No, Amanda, I can honestly say he wasn't. It just happened that gold was found on land he owned, and also emeralds, sapphires, garnets, and the rubies here, and mica. It just happened that way. He didn't go looking for it," Uncle John explained.

"Are all those other mines closed now?" Joe asked.

"No, not all of them," Uncle John answered. "We have a large mica mine over near Sylva, and we have a couple of other gem mines here in Macon County. They seem to be full of stones."

"If the rubies are in the gravel, how do you go about finding them? Do you just get down and dig through to the gravel?" Mandie asked.

Uncle John laughed. "No, dear, that would take forever. You have to remove the topsoil, and you need a water trough and a sieve. The loose dirt and fine gravel filter through the sieve and wash away, leaving the larger pieces of gravel in the sieve. Then you have to examine what's left to see if there are any rubies in it. Once in a while you'll find a ruby stuck in a rock left in the gravel."

"That sounds easy enough," Mandie said.

"Oh, but it takes time, lots of time, to do this and really come up with anything worthwhile. The rubies are few and far between," her uncle stated.

"And even though it sounds like fun, it's wet, dirty, back-breaking work," Dr. Woodard told her.

"But it'll be fun anyway," Joe remarked.

"Yes, I can't wait to get started. Are you getting us a water trough and a sieve, Uncle John?" Mandie asked.

"There's a trough already down there with a hand pump to bring the water through, and we've got sieves back at the house," Uncle John said. "While one of you dips the sieve in the water, the other one will have to be sure the water is pumping through."

"By the way, Amanda," Dr. Woodard warned, "the rubies you may find won't look like the setting in a ring. They'll be a dull, dirty-looking dark red. They have to be polished and cut before they are used in jewelry."

"That's right," Uncle John agreed. "You have to look very closely. Some of them might look just like old rocks."

"I'll be sure to examine every little particle," Mandie replied. "That way I'm sure I'll find some rubies."

"And if you do find one, what are you going to do with it?" her uncle asked.

Mandie's blue eyes sparkled as she thought for a moment and then answered, "Why, I'll have it polished and cut like Dr. Woodard said, and I'll have it made into something for my mother. That would make a nice Christmas present for her, wouldn't it?"

"It sure would. But in the meantime, I think you'd better plan on an alternate present because you might not find a single one, you know," Uncle John said.

"If there are any rubies down there, I'm sure Joe and

I will find them," Mandie replied, smiling.

"And what do you plan to do with any you find, Joe?" Uncle John asked.

"Me? You mean I can keep whatever I find?" Joe inquired.

"You certainly may. If you're going to do all that work, you're welcome to keep whatever you find," Uncle John told him.

"Well, thanks, Mr. Shaw. I'll just . . . uh . . . uh . . . keep them until I decide what to do with them, I suppose," the boy said, glancing shyly at Mandie.

"And don't you two forget," Uncle John reminded them, "I may be selling this mine to Jake Burns soon, so you'll have to work fast."

"When Sallie and Dimar get here, we'll have plenty of help," Mandie stated.

Just then one of the workmen stuck his head out of the opening to the mine. "Mr. Shaw," he called, "I reckon we'll have this thing safe and sound some time tomorrow."

"That's good, Boyd," John Shaw called back. "Then we'll let the kids explore it tomorrow." He walked on down to talk further with Boyd.

Mandie clasped her hands in delight, releasing Snowball onto her shoulder. He immediately jumped down and ran toward the workman.

"Thank goodness, it's not taking long to get it ready." Mandie turned to chase Snowball, and her bonnet fell back. "Snowball, come back here. Don't you go inside."

"I won't let him in, Missy," Boyd called to her as the white kitten raced on toward him.

Joe hurried to help. Together they cornered Snowball as he stopped to sniff at the workman. Mandie picked up the kitten and turned back up the hill. Joe followed.

"Snowball, you've got to learn to stop running away like that. One of these days you might get lost," Mandie reprimanded the kitten as she cuddled him in her arms.

"And then we'll have to waste time looking for him," Joe added.

"I know, and we don't have any time to waste. We have to go back to school after Thanksgiving, so we've got to hurry," Mandie agreed.

Dr. Woodard called to them as they came up the hill. "Do you see what I see?" He pointed to the trees behind him.

Mandie looked up the hill and then began running with Joe right beside her. Uncle Ned, Mandie's old Indian friend, was riding toward them on his horse.

As the old Cherokee dismounted and tied his horse to a tree, Mandie grabbed his wrinkled hand. "Uncle Ned, I'm so glad you got here. Did you bring Morning Star and everyone?" she asked excitedly.

Uncle Ned stooped to embrace the small girl. "Papoose, do not make talk so fast," he laughed. "Sallie and Dimar come with me. Morning Star come Thanksgiving Day. Needed in village now."

"I'm so glad you're here," Mandie said. She turned to Uncle John, who was coming up the hill with Dr. Woodard. "Are we going home now, Uncle John?"

"I suppose we are, Amanda," Uncle John told her. He extended his hand to the old Indian. "How are you, Uncle Ned?"

"Good," Uncle Ned replied.

Dr. Woodard shook hands with the Indian. "Glad to see you," he said.

Uncle John pointed to the opening in the mine.

"Looks like we'll have it open tomorrow, Uncle Ned."

"Bad to open," the old Indian grunted. "Ruby mine bad place."

Mandie and Joe looked at him and frowned.

"The workmen are making sure the timbers are solid and everything is safe," Uncle John assured him.

"No good mine. Your papa close. Bad to open," Uncle Ned insisted.

"What do you mean by bad?" Dr. Woodard asked.

"Your papa close mine because bad things happen. Bad to open mine," the Indian replied, adjusting the sling over his shoulder holding his bow and arrows.

"But why is it bad to open the mine?" Uncle John wanted to know.

"You no remember?"

"No, I was too young. What do you remember about it?" John persisted.

"I put away memory. Best not to open mine," Uncle Ned repeated.

"If you won't tell me why you think it shouldn't be opened, I don't see any reason not to," John said, exasperated.

Mandie took the old Indian's hand and gave it a slight jerk. "Please, Uncle Ned, tell us whatever you know."

"I watch over Papoose. I promise Jim Shaw when he go to happy hunting ground I watch over Papoose. When Papoose go in ruby mine I watch," he told the girl.

"My father would be proud of you, Uncle Ned, if he could know how well you've kept your promise since he died," Mandie responded.

Dr. Woodard cleared his throat. "All this talk of the mine being bad sounds awfully mysterious to me, Uncle

Ned," he said. "Is it safe for the young people to go inside?"

"I keep watch." Uncle Ned untied his horse. "Sallie and Dimar wait at house of John Shaw. They say hurry."

The others all looked at each other as the Indian mounted his horse and rode off. Then Mandie and Joe laughed loudly.

"We sure didn't get a straight answer from him," Mandie cried as she turned to get her pony. "Depend on Uncle Ned to keep a secret!"

"Yep, if anybody can keep a secret, he can," Joe added.

"Well, there's nothing left for us to do but go back to the house," Uncle John said to Dr. Woodard.

"Whatever was bothering Uncle Ned probably wasn't very important," Dr. Woodard agreed.

Uncle Ned was already out of sight by the time the others mounted. It wasn't far to John Shaw's house in the city of Franklin, and Mandie and Joe excitedly rushed ahead of the men.

As they approached the huge white house, they saw Sallie and Dimar sitting on the front porch waiting for them. Uncle Ned's horse stood at the gate, but the old Indian wasn't in sight. The young people quickly dismounted, tied up their ponies, and ran up the long walkway.

"Sallie! Dimar!" Mandie cried. "You finally got here!" She embraced Sallie Sweetwater, who was Uncle Ned's granddaughter, and turned to shake Dimar's hand. Dimar was a neighbor of the Sweetwaters.

"I am so excited!" Sallie laughed. "This is so different from where we live in Deep Creek."

"I know how you feel. I remember when Uncle Ned

helped me get here to Uncle John's house after my father died. I had never been away from our log cabin at Charley Gap." Mandie sat down beside Sallie in the swing. "But you have been here before."

"Yes, but it is exciting," the Indian girl said, smoothing her long black skirt.

Dimar cast an admiring glance at Mandie. "I am glad to see you, Mandie—and Joe, too," he said, sitting with Joe on a bench near the swing.

"Dimar, wait till you see the mine where we're going to hunt for rubies," Joe told him.

Mandie's blue eyes sparkled. "That's where we've just been. It'll be ready for us to go inside some time tomorrow."

"Inside?" the Indian boy questioned. "Ruby mines do not have an inside."

"This one does," Mandie replied. "Uncle John says the dirt was so deep they had to dig about nineteen feet down before they got to the gravel. We have to walk down some steps to get inside."

"Oh, I see," Dimar replied. "Then it will be interesting."

"According to Uncle Ned, it will be *bad*, but he wouldn't tell us what he meant by that," Joe added.

"Where is he?" Mandie asked. "He rode off ahead of us in a big hurry."

"He went inside the house," Sally answered. "He said that it is a bad mine and it should not be opened again."

"He would not tell us why," Dimar said.

Mandie rose from the swing. "Oh, well, Uncle John is getting it opened anyway. Let's go inside the house now."

Liza, the young Negro servant girl, appeared at the

front door. "Y'all wanted in de parlor," she said. "Ev'ry one of y'all."

"Thank you, Liza. We were just coming in," Mandie replied.

Liza stared at the two young Indians as the group entered the house and went through the big double doors into the parlor. She noticed every little detail as they passed her. Sallie, a little taller than Mandie, had black hair and black eyes. She had a red scarf tied around her hair, and shell beads jangled around the neck of her white blouse. Dimar wore a deerskin jacket like Uncle Ned's. He was not quite as tall as Joe, but he was handsome.

Mandie gave her mother a hug, spoke to Mrs. Woodard, and then sat down beside Uncle Ned. The others seated themselves in comfortable chairs around the room.

"I'm so glad you invited our friends for Thanksgiving," Mandie said to her mother. She looked up as Uncle John and Dr. Woodard entered the room.

Her mother smiled. "Your Grandmother Taft and Celia Hamilton will be here tomorrow," she said. "We will have a wonderful time."

Liza had followed the young people into the parlor and stood just inside the door, staring.

Elizabeth, Mandie's mother, noticed the servant girl and spoke to her. "Liza, would you please pass the little cakes for me while I pour the tea?"

"Yessum, Miz Shaw," Liza said, stepping forward to take the plate from her.

Elizabeth filled teacups and passed them around as Liza moved from one to another with the plate of sweetcakes. When she came to the Indians, she stood back and held out the plate.

"Liza, what's the matter with you?" Mandie asked. "You know all these people."

"Yessum, Missy. I jest ain't seed 'em in a long time," the Negro girl replied, quickly bringing the plate to Mandie.

"Liza, I think Aunt Lou needs your help getting the dinner table set. Why don't you go and see?" Elizabeth said.

"Yessum, yessum, Miz Shaw. I sho' bet she does," Liza replied quickly. She almost ran out the door.

Mrs. Woodard laughed. "That Liza is a strange one, isn't she, Elizabeth?"

"In a way. You know, she was born and raised here in this house and has never been anywhere else much."

"And she was already working here when you married John, wasn't she?" Mrs. Woodard asked.

"Yes, all the servants were here. I didn't make any staff changes when John and I got married. I just left everything the way it was. Aunt Lou is the best housekeeper anyone could ask for, and she keeps a rein on Liza and Jenny, the cook."

Uncle John took a sip of his tea and spoke to Elizabeth. "The mine will be ready to open tomorrow," he said.

Uncle Ned grunted, and everyone looked at him.

"Uncle Ned doesn't want us to open the mine at all," Mandie told her mother.

"Why not?" Elizabeth asked.

The old Indian merely shook his head.

"He said it's a bad mine," Mandie answered.

"A sad, bad mine," Uncle Ned corrected her.

"But why, Uncle Ned? What's wrong?" Elizabeth asked.

Uncle Ned crossed his arms and remained silent.

Elizabeth tried again. "Is it dangerous?"

When Uncle Ned didn't answer, John said, "I know it's safe. The workmen have been very careful to examine everything."

Mandie stood by Uncle Ned's chair and put her small white hand on the shoulder of his deerskin jacket. "Please tell us why you say the mine is a sad, bad mine," she begged.

Uncle Ned looked into her blue eyes and reached for her hand. "Papoose be all right. I watch over Papoose," he told her.

"And you won't tell us whatever you know?" Uncle John asked.

"You find out," the old Indian said.

Everyone fell silent, contemplating what the Indian had said. There was something very mysterious about the mine, and Mandie was determined to find out what it was.

Chapter 2 / The Store-bought Dress

When Uncle John and Dr. Woodard escorted the young people back to the mine the next day, Uncle Ned refused to come. He said they were only going to look inside and that when they really settled down to prospecting, then he would watch over Mandie and her friends.

The workmen were still at the mine when the group rode up.

Boyd came to meet John Shaw. "We had a little trouble getting some new posts cut just the right height, Mr. Shaw," he said. "So I guess it'll be a while yet before we're through. I'm sorry."

"That's all right, Boyd. Take time to be sure it's positively safe. Don't rush and cut corners," John Shaw told him.

"That's why we've been this long getting it open. I know how important it is to know without a doubt that it's safe for the young people," Boyd said.

Dimar sat forward on his pony and smiled at Mandie. "Now I understand why you said it had an inside, Mandie," he said.

"Uncle John said it's probably nineteen feet deep under there," Mandie explained.

The Indian boy looked around. "The dirt from uphill there has probably washed down this way for a hundred years or more. That is why the gravel was so far down."

Sallie followed his gaze. "I see a chimney over there," she said, pointing off through the dense trees that were beginning to lose their leaves. "Does someone live there?"

"Let's go see while we're waiting for them to get finished," Mandie said. She called to Uncle John and Dr. Woodard, who were still talking to Boyd. "We're going to ride over there through the trees." She pointed.

"Don't go too far away," Uncle John called back.

"And don't be gone too long," Dr. Woodard added.

The young people promised they wouldn't and rode off through the trees in the direction of the chimney.

Coming into a clearing a few hundred yards away, they found an old abandoned farmhouse, standing on tall stone pillars. The shutters hung haphazardly from the windows, and the front door stood half open. Tall weeds surrounded the house.

Joe slid off his pony beside the sagging front porch. "Looks like nobody lives here," he remarked.

The others dismounted and joined him as he carefully stepped up the shaky front porch steps.

"I wonder if this house is on Uncle John's property," Mandie said as she and the two young Indians followed.

"It is so near the mine it probably belongs to your Uncle John," Dimar said, looking back the direction they had come.

"This is a very old, very worn-out house. We must be

careful. Something may fall in," Sallie cautioned the others as she looked about.

Joe stepped up to the front door, which was slightly ajar, and pushed it open. "The inside seems to be all right." He walked into the long front room of the house. At one end rose the huge fireplace for the chimney they had seen.

The others followed Joe inside. Mandie stepped through the doorway into another room. There was something hanging on the far wall. She walked over to it. "Look what I've found!" she exclaimed. "A lady's dress! And it must be store-bought! Look!"

She took the garment from the nail and held it up for all to see. It was a light blue gingham dress with white frills and buttons. Around the waist was a wide sash.

Sallie held the material up to her nose. "It is new," she said. "I can smell the starch in the new cloth."

"It looks just like something in the Sears Roebuck catalogue," Joe said, watching the girls examine the dress.

Dimar laughed. "Yes, it must be a white lady's dress. No Cherokee could afford a store-bought dress like that."

Mandie puzzled over the matter. "Who do you suppose would leave a pretty, new dress in this old falling-down house?"

"Maybe whoever lived here last," Joe suggested.

"I do not think so," Sallie said. "This house looks like it has been deserted a long time, and that dress is fresh and new."

Joe climbed the ladder and stuck his head into the attic room. "Nothing up here," he called down to the others. "When the people moved out of here, whoever they were, they sure didn't leave anything behind."

The others looked around downstairs.

Dimar walked over to the huge open fireplace. "There are not even any ashes left in the fireplace," he said.

"What should we do with this dress?" Mandie asked, still holding it in her arms.

"Leave it where you found it," Joe said, coming back down the ladder. "It's not ours."

"It seems a shame to leave such a pretty dress in this dirty old house, but I suppose you're right," Mandie reluctantly agreed. She turned to hang the dress and sash back on the nail.

"Whoever left it here will be sure to return to get it," Dimar stated.

"I know, and we'll never know whose it is," Mandie said, regretfully.

Joe walked over and stood in front of Mandie. He drew himself up to his full gangly height and snapped his galluses with his thumbs. "Mandie, this dress is none of our business. Now please don't go off on one of your investigating adventures because I won't help you," he told her.

"Joe Woodard, you think I make a mystery out of everything. Well, I don't," Mandie replied, stomping her foot.

Sallie, always the peacemaker, spoke up quickly. "I think we should go," she said. "Your uncle will be looking for us if we are gone too long. Besides, they may have the mine open by now."

"You're right, Sallie. We'd better get back," Mandie agreed, hurrying toward the door.

Without another word the young people rode back to join Uncle John and Dr. Woodard at the mine.

"Boyd needs the rest of the day to get the new posts in," Uncle John told them.

The four moaned in protest.

"I know you are all disappointed, but at least we'll know the place is safe once Boyd gets done with it," Uncle John said. "He should be finished tomorrow."

"I sure hope so," Mandie said.

"Yeah, our holidays are going away fast," Joe added. He paused for a moment, then looked up at Mandie's uncle. "Mr. Shaw, how long has it been since someone lived in that old house over there?"

"Why, I don't remember. It seems like someone lived there when I was a child, but I'm not sure," John replied.

"Does that house belong to you, Uncle John?" Mandie asked.

"It's on our land. We have several hundred acres through here," Uncle John answered. "Why? Did you see someone over there?"

"No, sir," Mandie said. "But we found a brand-new dress hanging on a nail in one of the rooms of that house."

John Shaw and Dr. Woodard looked at each other in surprise.

"You found a new dress in there?" Uncle John questioned. "That's strange."

"Maybe someone is using the house, John," Dr. Woodard suggested.

"No, sir, it's completely empty, not even any ashes in the fireplace," Joe put in.

"Did you leave the dress where you found it?" Uncle John asked.

"Yes, sir. I put it back on the nail," Mandie replied.

"Well, it's not hurting anything, so we'll just leave it where it is," Uncle John told the young people. "Now we'd better get home and see if the rest of our company has arrived."

The young people raced their ponies ahead of the men and pulled up in front of John Shaw's house. Mandie's heart beat wildly as she recognized her Grandmother Taft's carriage parked at the gate. Mandie and her friends quickly tied up their ponies at the hitching post and rushed up the front steps.

"Celia!" Mandie cried, embracing the auburn-haired girl on the porch as though she hadn't seen her in months. Actually, they had parted only the week before at the Misses Heathwood's School in Asheville. The school closed for the Thanksgiving holidays. Celia had gone home to Richmond. Then her mother had brought her back to Mrs. Taft's house in Asheville so Celia could go on to Mandie's house in Franklin with Mrs. Taft.

Mandie turned to the boys. "Joe, will you and Dimar wait for us in the sun-room? We'll take Celia upstairs so she can get freshened up. Mother and the others are probably in the parlor."

The boys agreed and the girls rushed up the stairs to Mandie's bedroom where another bed had been moved in so that Mandie, Sallie, and Celia could share a room. There in the middle of Mandie's bed was Snowball, curled up asleep. He opened his blue eyes sleepily and stood up, stretching. He sat there washing his face and watching the girls.

Celia pulled off her bonnet and gloves that matched her brown traveling suit. She danced about the room, looking at everything. "Oh, I love your Uncle John's house," she said. "It's beautiful! And Sallie, I'm so glad to finally get a chance to know you. Mandie talks about you all the time at that school we go to in Asheville."

"And I am glad to make your acquaintance, Celia. Mandie talks about you a lot, too. Mandie is my dearest friend, and I hope she will soon be able to visit us for a long stay. Every time she visits they do not have much time. Maybe next summer when school is out, you could come with Mandie for a long visit," Sallie invited.

"I'd love to, Sallie. Let's plan on it, provided my mother gives me permission," Celia replied. Looking around, she spied her luggage in a corner. "Let me take off this traveling outfit and put on some more comfortable clothes." She opened the nearest bag and pulled out a green calico dress.

"I'll help you hang your things in the wardrobe with Sallie's and mine," Mandie offered, stooping to unpack while Celia changed clothes.

With Sallie's help, they were soon finished, and the three girls hurried downstairs again.

Mandie began to laugh. "I just realized something," she said. "I got so excited about seeing you, Celia, that I forgot to even say hello to my Grandmother Taft."

The other girls giggled with her. At the bottom of the steps, they ran into Aunt Lou, the robust Negro housekeeper, who at that moment was wiping her round face on her big white apron.

Mandie started to introduce Celia. "Aunt Lou, this is—"

"Slow down, my chile," the black woman scolded with a twinkle in her eye. "I bet you don't know who be in de parlor."

"Yes, I do, Aunt Lou," Mandie replied in a teasing voice. "It's Grandmother Taft."

Aunt Lou pouted. "Yo' Gramma Taft and who else?" she teased back.

Mandie's eyes grew wide. "I don't know, Aunt Lou. Who is it?"

The Negro woman looked up at the ceiling. "Some girl whut ain't got a lick o' sense," she replied.

"Hilda?" Mandie grabbed Celia's and Sallie's hands. "Come on!" She led the way into the parlor and ran to hug her grandmother. There on the settee beside Mrs. Taft sat Hilda Edney, the poor girl Mandie and Celia had found hiding in the attic of their school. But now here she was, dressed like a millionaire's daughter.

Joe and Dimar in the sun-room heard the commotion and came into the room. Everyone started to talk at once.

Hilda, seeing Mandie, jumped up, stood right in front of her, and extended her hand, smiling. "I . . . love . . . you." She enunciated each word slowly.

"Oh, Hilda, I love you, too," Mandie said, putting her arms around the girl. "And you are talking more and more."

Hilda burst into tears and clung to Mandie.

Mrs. Taft stood and patted Hilda on the shoulder. "There, there, now. What is it, dear?"

The dark-haired girl just kept crying and wouldn't let go of Mandie.

"Hilda," Mandie tried to scold the girl gently. "Let's sit down over there. There's nothing to cry about. Young ladies don't cry in front of other people."

Hilda allowed herself to be led to the settee, and she sat down beside Mandie.

Mrs. Taft looked concerned. "I think Hilda is afraid she won't ever see you again if the Pattons adopt her. She seems frightened of them."

"Hilda, the Pattons are real nice people. And they live

down in Charleston where you can see the ocean," Mandie told her.

"No!" Hilda sobbed. "No!" She reached for Mandie's hand and squeezed it tightly.

"Grandmother, how did you happen to bring Hilda here?" Mandie asked.

"Dear, when the Pattons came to get Hilda from the sanitarium, she was gone. They couldn't find her anywhere. Then Aunt Phoebe at your school sent word to me that Hilda was at their home," Mrs. Taft explained. "I had to go get her, and when I tried to take her back to the sanitarium, she became wild. So I thought I would just bring her here to see you. Since she loves you so much, maybe you can talk some sense into her head."

"I doubt if I can, Grandmother. Hilda doesn't understand everything we say," Mandie said.

Dr. Woodard cleared his throat. "She understands more than you think she does. And she is improving all the time. After being shut away in that room by herself most of her life simply because she couldn't talk, I think she is doing well."

Hilda had hushed and was listening carefully to Dr. Woodard. He visited her often at the sanitarium, and she seemed to like him.

Mandie turned to Hilda, smiling. "Just wait until you see the ruby mine Uncle John owns," she said, changing the subject abruptly. "He's going to let us dig in it and look for rubies. And you can help if you don't cry anymore."

Hilda brushed the back of her hand across her wet eyes. Mrs. Taft handed her a handkerchief, and Hilda wiped her eyes with it. Straightening, she smiled at Mandie. "Help. I help," she said, though not seemingly aware of what the conversation was all about.

Mandie smiled back at her and then fingered Hilda's lovely lavender silk dress. "Where did you get the pretty dress?" she asked.

Hilda looked down, then quickly stood up to shake out her long full skirt. Her brown eyes shone as she tossed her long dark hair. "Gramma," she said, pointing to Mrs. Taft. "Gramma."

Mandie looked at her Grandmother Taft.

"Yes, dear, I had to get her some clothes to take with her to the Pattons. I've been her benefactor ever since you and Celia found her," Mrs. Taft reminded Mandie.

Sallie drew in a deep breath and whispered to Celia, "So this is the girl you and Mandie found hiding in the attic at your school."

"Yes, isn't she pretty?" Celia replied.

"She is," Sallie agreed.

"What are you going to do about her, Mrs. Taft?" Dr. Woodard asked. "You know how much the Pattons want to take her into their home."

"I know, but if she's frightened, maybe she could stay with me in my home for a while," Mrs. Taft told him. "As you know, I have plenty of room."

"Hilda? Staying with you, Mother?" Elizabeth spoke up.

"Why, yes, what's wrong with that?" Mrs. Taft asked.

"Nothing, except that you like to travel all over, and you're not used to having a young person around," Elizabeth replied.

"Well, I did have a young person around when you were growing up," Mrs. Taft said. "If I can teach her some manners, maybe I'll take her with me on some of my other travels."

Everyone looked at each other and then at Hilda, who was silently examining the material of her dress.

Suddenly Mandie laughed loudly. "Oh, Grandmother! If anyone could teach her some manners, you could! You always end up doing the impossible."

"We'll see," Mrs. Taft said. "Besides, when you and Celia go back to school, you can spend a lot of time over at my house helping me teach her."

"I'll be glad to help, Mrs. Taft," Celia offered.

"I'm so glad you live in Asheville, Grandmother," Mandie said. "That's the only good part about going to that school so far from home."

"And I'm glad you're near me during school, dear," Mrs. Taft said with a mischievous smile. "Now what about this ruby mine y'all are going to explore?"

Mandie's eyes lit up. "It's going to be fun," she said. "It's a big hole in the ground, and I'm sure there are still rubies in it. Uncle John's going to show us how to look for them, and he says we can keep any rubies we find!"

"That does sound like fun," Mrs. Taft replied.

"It would be nice of you to take Hilda with y'all when you go to dig in the mine," Dr. Woodard said. "I know she'll be fascinated by it."

"Do you think it'll be all right for Hilda to go?" Uncle John asked. "Mightn't she get into something and get hurt?"

"No, I think Mandie will be able to control her," Dr. Woodard replied.

"Tell me about the mine, please," Celia begged.

"It's just a great big hole in the ground," Joe teased.

"Are you sure the mine is safe?" Mrs. Taft asked.

"I'm having workmen go over every inch of it before

the young people will be allowed inside," John assured her.

Elizabeth bristled. "Mother, you know John and I would never allow Amanda to go if it weren't safe."

"Yes, of course, dear," Mrs. Taft replied.

Later that night, when Elizabeth told the girls it was time to go to bed, Mandie didn't protest.

"All right, Mother." She yawned. "I guess it has been a long day." She turned to Hilda. "You are to sleep in the room with Celia, Sallie and me," she said. "Let's go upstairs."

Saying good night to everyone, the girls went up to Mandie's room. Mandie pulled a trundle bed out from under her bed and showed it to Hilda. "You sleep on this," she said.

Hilda stood watching, not saying a word. It took a lot of coaxing from the other three girls to get Hilda to undress for bed. When they finally got her to lie down in the trundle bed, Hilda held onto the covers and watched every move the others made as they finished getting ready for bed.

"Do you think she'll stay there to sleep?" Sallie asked doubtfully.

"I think so. Anyway, I'll hear her if she gets up during the night," Mandie answered.

But Mandie slept soundly that night and didn't hear a thing.

Chapter 3 / Waiting

Mandie awoke early, just about dawn, and when she opened her eyes, the trundle bed was empty. She sat up quickly, disturbing Snowball who was sleeping at her feet.

Where was Hilda?

Sallie stirred in her bed and sat up.

"Hilda is gone!" Mandie whispered.

Sallie blinked her eyes a few times and looked around the room. "We must find her," the Indian girl said, swinging her feet out of bed onto the floor.

Mandie crawled over the trundle bed and stood up. "There's no telling where Hilda is," she said, pulling her robe on over her long nightgown. "Come on," she whispered in order not to wake Celia.

Snowball jumped down from the bed and stretched, watching his mistress.

Sallie quickly threw on her robe and slippers, and the two girls started toward the door.

Suddenly the door came open and Hilda walked in, followed by Liza.

"Case y'all been lookin' fo' dis Hilda girl, she been sleepin' in my bed," Liza told them.

Taking one look at Mandie, Hilda went straight to the trundle bed and jumped in, pulling the covers over her.

"In *your* bed, Liza?" Mandie asked, astonished.

"In de middle o' de night I heerd somethin', and here she wuz gittin' in de other side o' my bed. She didn't say a word, jes' got under de covers and went straight to sleep," Liza explained.

"I wonder how she knew where Liza was," Sallie said.

"I don't rightly know, Missy," Liza told them. "I told her she had to come back up here 'cause I has to git down to de kitchen."

"I'm sorry, Liza. I'll try to keep her here tonight," Mandie said.

"Dat's all right, Missy. I don't care if she wants to sleep in my bed, long as she don't kick," Liza said.

Mandie and Sallie laughed.

Celia awoke and sat up, rubbing her eyes and looking around. "As long as who doesn't kick?" she asked, yawning sleepily.

"Hilda sneaked off during the night and slept with Liza," Mandie explained.

"I gotta go, Missy. Gotta help git breakfus'," Liza said, dancing over to the door. "I knows she don't know no better, so don't y'all be mean to her." Liza rushed out of the room.

"Sorry we woke you, Celia," Mandie apologized.

Celia swung her feet onto the carpet and stood up, stretching. "That's all right. I'm hungry anyway, and Liza said she was going to cook breakfast," she replied. "I don't want to miss that."

"All right, let's get dressed and go down to the kitchen," Mandie suggested.

"That is a good idea," Sallie agreed. "But what about Hilda?"

The girls looked at Hilda in the trundle bed. She was either fast asleep or was making a good pretense of it.

"Let's just leave her here," Mandie said. "I don't think she wants to get up right now."

The three girls washed their faces quickly and slipped into their dresses, being careful not to disturb Hilda. After they brushed their hair, Mandie picked up Snowball, and they tiptoed out of the room.

As Celia silently closed the door behind them, Hilda opened one eye to see that they were gone, then jumped up and quickly put on her dress and shoes. Taking Mandie's shawl from the wardrobe, she threw it around her shoulders, opened the door, and listened. Hearing nothing, she stepped into the hallway and paused again. Then she tiptoed down the servants' stairway at the end of the hallway. Making her way through the dimly lighted hallway downstairs, she found the back door, opened it, and ran out into the yard and off through the shrubbery.

Although Mandie and her two friends stood right inside the kitchen near the back door, they didn't hear her leave.

Aunt Lou was stacking plates on the table while Jenny, the cook, tended something on the big black cookstove and Liza folded napkins.

"Whut fo' you girls done got up so early?" Aunt Lou asked them.

"Please, Aunt Lou, let us eat here in the kitchen," Mandie begged. "It'll be a long time before the grownups get up, and we're starving to death."

"And I s'pose dem boys dey'll be comin' to de kitchen, too," Aunt Lou fussed.

"I don't know whether they're awake yet or not," Mandie told her.

"They are," came a loud voice behind them. "We're hungry, too."

The girls turned to find Joe and Dimar standing just inside the doorway, listening to their conversation.

"Now, my chile, I ain't said y'all could eat in here," Aunt Lou said, " 'cause y'all ain't told me why y'all got up so early."

"It was because of Hilda," Celia volunteered.

Aunt Lou put her hands on her broad hips as she straightened up. "Dat Hilda girl?"

"Yes. Hilda slept in Liza's bed last night," Mandie said. "She slipped out of my room after we went to sleep."

Aunt Lou looked from Mandie to Liza, who grinned and kept on with her task. "Liza, why didn't you make dat girl go back where she belong?" Aunt Lou asked.

"She ain't right in de haid so I didn't wanta be mean to huh," Liza replied.

"She ain't right in de haid 'cause nobody don't try to teach huh no sense," Aunt Lou said.

"We've been trying to, Aunt Lou," Mandie said. "She's learning. It's slow, but she is learning."

"Dr. Woodard says she is brighter than we think she is," Sallie added.

"That's right," Joe agreed.

"And where be dat Hilda girl now?" Aunt Lou asked.

"Liza brought her back to my room a while ago. She's asleep on the trundle bed," Mandie explained.

Aunt Lou shook her head. "I still cain't let y'all eat yet, 'cause breakfus' ain't ready," she said, exasperated. "Y'all find somethin' else to do till we's ready."

Mandie looked at her friends. "What shall we do until breakfast?" she asked them.

"I haven't seen the tunnel yet," Celia said. "You've always talked about the tunnel in this house. I'd like to see it."

"We could do that this morning," Mandie said. "I know the rest of you have been through it, but it won't take long to show it to Celia."

The others agreed enthusiastically, and Mandie led them out of the kitchen and down the hall toward the stairs. As they passed the parlor, Mandie heard a noise and peeked in. There sat Uncle John, quietly reading the newspaper by the window. She went in to speak to him, and the others followed.

"Why are you up so early, Uncle John?" she asked.

"I don't know," he said. "Something woke me before dawn, and I couldn't get back to sleep. What are you all up to already?"

"We want to show Celia the secret tunnel," Mandie answered.

Uncle John's face grew sober, and he stood up. He folded the newspaper and laid it on the table. "I'd like to talk to you alone, Amanda, before you go through the tunnel," Uncle John told her.

Everyone looked at Mandie, questioningly.

"This is a personal matter between Amanda and me. It won't take long," he said.

"All right, Uncle John," Mandie replied. "Will the rest of you wait for me here in the parlor for a few minutes?"

They all nodded.

What have I done now? she wondered. If Uncle John needed to have a private conversation with her, it must be something bad, she reasoned.

Uncle John laughed. "Don't look so worried, Amanda. I'm not going to spank you."

Everyone laughed. Mandie drew a breath of relief.

"Let's go upstairs," Uncle John suggested as they started to leave the parlor.

Mandie followed her uncle from the room. "Upstairs?" she questioned.

He led her up the steps to the door of the third floor library. There he paused with his hand on the doorknob. "I don't know whether I ever told you or not, but this room was my mother's favorite place in this house. She came here to think and solve problems, and to read all our many wonderful books," he said.

"You told me she was a beautiful young Indian girl when your father married her," Mandie replied.

Uncle John slowly opened the door. "Yes, she never lived to grow old," he said sadly, pushing the door open wide.

Immediately in front of them, across the length of the room was a huge fireplace. Over that hung a portrait that had not been there before.

Mandie rushed forward. "My Grandmother Shaw!" she cried. "Oh, she was so beautiful!"

Tears moistened Mandie's blue eyes as she stared at the likeness of a beautiful Indian girl looking down at her. The girl was dressed in red silk; her thick black hair piled high on her head. Indian beads sparkled on her ears, and at her throat they were entwined with a red ribbon.

"She looks as though she could see us and could speak," Mandie said softly.

Uncle John nodded and put an arm around his stepdaughter. "I had told you this portrait was in Asheville getting the frame refinished, remember? I just got it back last week, and I wanted you to see it alone with me," he told her.

Mandie reached up to grasp his hand on her shoulder. "Thank you, Uncle John, for knowing how important this moment is to me. I wish I could have known her," she said with a quiver in her voice.

"Yes, well, even your father was too young to remember her. She died when Jim was only a few months old, but since I was fifteen years older than your father, I can remember her well. She was beautiful, always happy, full of life, always doing things for other people. And she and my father were so much in love. After she died, my father just wasted away. He died in 1868, as you know, when your father was only five years old."

Mandie turned to face him. "And my father died so young, Uncle John. He was just barely thirty-seven years old."

Uncle John tightened his arm around her. "I know, dear. Only God knows the answer to our sorrows."

Mandie wiped tears from her eyes with the back of her hand and looked up at her uncle. "I thank God every night in my prayers for helping me to find you and my real mother after my father died," Mandie said. "And I would never have agreed to anyone but you marrying my mother and becoming my stepfather."

"Yes, I suppose you would have given an unwanted stepfather a bad time," Uncle John teased her, smoothing her long blonde hair.

"You know me!" Mandie laughed.

"Now I think you'd better get back to your friends. I've left the door unlocked over there for you," Uncle John told her, pointing to a small door at one side of the room. "I knew you would want to show Celia the tunnel."

"Thanks, Uncle John. I love you," Mandie said. Squeezing his hand tightly, she hurried back to the other young people and found them impatiently waiting for her in the parlor. Snowball was curled up in the middle of the carpet.

"Are you ready now?" Mandie asked.

"Are *you* ready?" Joe laughed.

"Yes, I had a nice surprise just now. I'll show you when we get up there," Mandie promised.

"Step this way, ladies and gent," Joe teased as he rose to lead the way. "We've all been there before except Celia, so you know the way."

Celia, Sallie, and Dimar followed Joe and Mandie up the stairs to the third floor. They hurried down the long hallway to the door to the library where Mandie had just been.

As they stepped into the room, Mandie pointed to the portrait. "That's what Uncle John wanted to show me," she told her friends. "He just got it back from being re-finished. I had never seen it before. It's my Grandmother Shaw—my father's mother, and Uncle John's mother, too, of course."

The group paused to admire the portrait.

Mandie turned toward the small door that Uncle John had left unlocked. "Joe, would you please carry that lamp over there?" she asked.

Joe picked up the lamp from a nearby table and lighted it.

As Mandie opened the door, Celia stood directly behind her. "It looks just like a closet with a paneled wall, doesn't it?" Mandie stood to one side to let Celia look closely. Then Mandie continued. "Watch what happens when I push this." She pushed the latch, and the paneled wall swung around, making a doorway.

Celia caught her breath in astonishment.

"Now we go right through here," Joe said as he stepped through the doorway into the tunnel.

Celia held onto Mandie's hand as they walked down a dark hallway illuminated only by the oil lamp. The others followed. They went down, down, down the dark stairs to a short hallway below where there were more stairs and another door.

They kept on through doors and down stairways until Joe stopped at a door at the end of a hallway.

"Whew!" Celia gasped. "This is something!"

"My great-grandfather built this house about the time the Cherokees were being moved out of North Carolina. He didn't believe in the white people's cruelty toward the Indians, and he hid dozens of the Cherokees in this tunnel and fed and clothed them until about 1842 when it was safe for them to go out and set up living quarters elsewhere," Mandie explained. "That was the way my grandfather met my grandmother. He was twenty-eight, and she was just eighteen. She was a beautiful young Indian girl, as you can tell from that portrait in the library."

"What a love story!" Celia exclaimed.

"Sallie's grandfather, whom we all call Uncle Ned, knew all about this tunnel and never told me about it," said Mandie. "One day I accidentally stumbled into the wall upstairs with Polly, my friend nextdoor, when the wall opened up and we found the tunnel."

"My grandfather can keep a secret," remarked Sallie. "He never told me about the tunnel either."

"This is unbelievable," Celia said, shaking her auburn curls. "Imagine having to live in this tunnel for such a long time. It must have been terrible!"

"Yes, for a Cherokee to have to be confined must have been almost like death," Dimar said. "The Cherokee likes to be free as a bird with no cage."

"And now when I open this door, Celia," Joe teased, "you will be surprised to see what awaits you." Reaching for the key on a nail, he inserted it in the lock, turned it, and pulled the door open, deliberately slow.

There, outside the door, stood Hilda, just as surprised as the rest of the young people.

"That's n-not what I had in mind," Joe stammered. "I meant the outdoors."

"Hilda! What are you doing out here?" Mandie asked, stepping out into the sunshine. She squinted her eyes to adjust to the brightness.

"We thought you were upstairs in bed," Sallie said. "How did you get out here?"

"She has a mind of her own," Dimar observed.

As the others stepped out of the tunnel, they shivered in the chilly morning air.

"Brrrr! I am cold!" Celia rubbed her arms lightly. "Hilda is smarter than we are. She is at least wearing a shawl."

"Yes, my shawl," Mandie laughed.

Joe shuffled through the newly fallen leaves near the tunnel entrance. "It's getting on toward wintertime," he said.

"Come on, Hilda," Mandie urged. "It's time to eat."

Hilda smiled at Mandie. "Eat," she repeated.

"She is learning," Dimar said.

"We just have to keep teaching her," Mandie replied.

"I think we should go around the outside of the house to take her inside," Joe suggested. "That dark tunnel might scare her."

The others agreed.

"I'll run back through the tunnel and lock it so I can leave the lamp upstairs. I'll catch up with you," Joe said.

Joe disappeared inside and the others hurried through the back door.

Liza stood near the sideboard, ready to pour coffee. She grinned when they entered the breakfast room with Hilda. "What fun!" She laughed.

"Yeah, fun, before breakfast," grumbled Joe as he picked up a plate. "Umm! Everything smells so good!"

Mandie removed the shawl from Hilda's shoulders and placed it on a chair at the table.

"Now, Hilda, come and get yourself a plate and fill it up with food," Mandie told the girl. Leading her to the stack of china, she handed Hilda a plate.

Hilda looked at the empty plate and started to hand it back.

"No!" Mandie commanded, taking a plate for herself. "You fill it up like this." Mandie began putting food on her own plate, then reached to put some on Hilda's.

The girl seemed to understand. She immediately started piling food on her plate.

"Not too much of one thing," Mandie told her. "The plate won't hold so much. You see, you take a little of whatever you want now, and then you can come back and get more if you want it."

"Little." Hilda repeated the word, then began taking a very small amount of grits.

"That's the way." Mandie guided her down the length of the sideboard as they both took a small portion of various foods.

Joe watched the two of them for a few minutes, then whispered to Mandie, "You plan to take her along with us to the mine? Can you imagine how much trouble she'll be?"

"That's the only way to teach her anything. We have to let her participate in whatever we do," Mandie replied.

"Just remember that it was your idea," Joe remarked.

Suddenly Hilda grabbed Dimar's hand. "Come!" she said, pulling him toward the table. She balanced her plate precariously with her other hand.

Dimar looked confused, but since he had already filled his plate, he let her lead him.

Everyone looked at each other.

"She seems to like you, Dimar," Joe teased.

"She can't say much, but she knows how to let you know when she likes something," Mandie said.

"Maybe I can teach her to speak Cherokee," Dimar said, sitting down at the table with Hilda.

The others stood still for a moment, then everyone burst out laughing. This was going to be interesting.

Chapter 4 / Another Secret Tunnel

"I'm not going with y'all, this afternoon," Uncle John told the young people at the noontime meal later that day. "We grown folks are all going over to visit the Hadleys, and we won't be back until time for supper. I trust you all to behave and not to do anything you shouldn't. The men should be already gone from the mine, and you may go inside to look, but you'll have to wait to search for rubies until I can show you how."

Mandie looked down the long dining table at her old Indian friend. "Uncle Ned, aren't you going with us?" she asked.

"No, Papoose. John Shaw want me see Hadleys," the Indian replied.

"You may take Liza if you think you need help in looking after Hilda," Elizabeth said.

"I will look after Hilda," Dimar offered. "I am teaching her Cherokee."

Mandie, Celia, and Sallie looked at each other and smiled. Joe nudged Dimar and grinned.

"Please don't let her get away from you, Dimar," Elizabeth cautioned. "She likes to run away at times."

"We know," the girls said in unison, giggling.

"She will not run away from me," Dimar replied.

As everyone rose from the table, the old Indian stopped the young people.

"Papooses be good," Uncle Ned told the girls. "Boys, behave."

"We will," they all promised.

"I'm sure these nice young people will be fine," said Grandmother Taft. "I'd say there's not a bad one in the lot. But just in case you need us, Amanda, you know where the Hadleys live on the other side of town."

"No, Grandmother, I don't know the Hadleys," Mandie replied. "I'm at school in Asheville so much that I don't know many people in Franklin."

"I know where they live," Joe said. "I go over there with my father sometimes when they need doctoring. They're older people."

"Well, that's where we will be," Mrs. Taft said.

"All right. Let's go!" Joe urged.

"Goodbye, Mother," Mandie called as the young people left the room.

Jason Bond had brought ponies to the gate for them and was waiting with lanterns and matches. "Here. You'll be needin' these." He handed the lanterns to the boys and gave the matches to the girls. "Y'all be careful now. Just leave the ponies here when you come back, and I'll put them away."

"Thank you, Mr. Jason." Mandie put Snowball on her shoulder. "Don't you want to come with us?" she asked the caretaker.

"Nope. I'm not interested in that hole in the ground," he said.

"But there may be rubies in it," Joe told him.

"There may be and there may not be. It's not worth all that hard work to find out for sure," the caretaker replied. "I'll be here when you get back."

The young people waved goodbye and rushed to the mine. Dimar rode close to Hilda, who seemed to be enjoying the journey.

Mandie looked at Joe. "Let's go by the old house first and show everybody that dress," she suggested, turning her pony in that direction.

The others followed. At the front steps of the old farmhouse, they all dismounted except Hilda. Since she refused to get down from her pony, Dimar stayed outside with her.

"Whose house is this?" Celia asked, following the others inside.

"It belongs to Uncle John, but no one has lived in it for a long, long time," Mandie told her friend. She rushed into the next room to look for the dress.

"It's gone!" cried Mandie and Sallie together, staring at the nail where the dress had hung.

"I told you whoever it belonged to would come back and get it," Joe reminded them.

"Was it a pretty dress? What color was it?" Celia asked.

"It was pretty—" Mandie answered, shifting Snowball from one shoulder to the other, "—a blue gingham, store-bought dress with a sash."

"Well, don't worry about that dress," Joe said. "Let's get on over to the mine." He led the way out of the house and back to their ponies.

As they approached the mine, Celia pointed to the planks covering the ground. "What are all those boards doing there?" she asked.

"They make a roof for the mine," Mandie said. "Come on." She jumped down from her pony and tied him to a branch. "The steps are over here." Taking the lead, she gave Joe and Dimar the matches. "You'd better light the lanterns. It's probably dark down there."

"I'm sure it is. There aren't any windows, you know," Joe replied, lighting the lantern. "Let me go first with the light."

"Then I'll light mine and follow behind," said Dimar.

The others followed Joe down the steep steps into the underground cavern. Hilda clung to Dimar's hand, not understanding what was going on.

Joe flashed the lantern around as they inspected the place. There was a water trough descending through one side. The ground was uneven, mostly gravel and rocks. A number of shovels, hoes, and picks stood in one corner.

"Everything is neat and in order," Sallie remarked.

"Yes, the men did a good job of cleaning up the place," Mandie agreed, setting Snowball down. "Now don't run away, Snowball. I don't think there's anywhere to go down here except back up the steps."

The kitten played around with the bristles of a home-made broom leaning against a nearby post in the corner.

"Well, where are the rubies?" Celia asked.

"You have to dig for them," Joe told her.

"Dig?" she questioned.

"Of course. They aren't just laying around loose in plain sight," Mandie replied.

The young people looked around for several minutes; then suddenly Sallie spoke up. "Where is Snowball?" she asked. "I do not see him anywhere."

Immediately everyone scrambled around, looking for the white kitten.

"He must have gone up the steps," Mandie said, starting toward the steps where Dimar and Hilda were standing.

"He did not go up there. I would have seen him," Dimar said.

"But that's the only way out of here, and I sure don't see him anywhere else," Joe said, flashing the lantern around.

Dimar carefully searched around the posts.

"Snowball was playing with that broom, remember?" Celia said, walking toward the corner. Mandie and Sallie followed her.

Sallie stopped short, pointing. "Look! There is a passageway going out of here," she said.

Joe and Dimar came quickly with the lanterns and lit up the area. Sallie was right. There was a corridor leading into the darkness beyond. A pile of timbers lay nearby.

"Then Snowball must have gone that way," Mandie said. "Come on with the lanterns. I'm going to look for him."

Joe led the way into the tunnel, lighting it with the lantern. It seemed to be a narrow dirt tunnel with posts here and there holding it up.

"Snowball! Here kitty, kitty!" Mandie called as she went along.

The others followed, and Hilda clung to Dimar in fright as he led her into the tunnel.

"Oh, what places y'all can get involved in!" Celia gasped.

"Where do you suppose this tunnel goes?" Dimar asked, holding his lantern a little higher.

"I don't know. Uncle John didn't mention this tunnel," Mandie replied. "Snowball! Here, kitty!" She strained her eyes to look for the kitten in the dim light.

As they turned a bend in the tunnel, Joe called back to the others. "I see daylight ahead!" he exclaimed, hurrying forward.

The others rushed to keep up with him. As they approached the opening at the end of the tunnel, Joe blew out his lantern and Dimar did likewise. Rose Creek, a branch of the Little Tennessee River, ran a short distance from the tunnel, and there, playing near the water, was Snowball.

Mandie ran and snatched up the kitten. "Snowball, you've been bad!" she scolded. "You know you aren't supposed to run away!" She held him up to look into his face.

Snowball meowed in reply and reached for her shoulder with his tiny paws.

"Ah, Snowball, you're full of stickers," she cried. Then gently and carefully she began removing the briars, stroking his fur as she worked. As she did that, Mandie caught sight of something blue laying on the ground nearby. She quickly picked it up.

"Look!" she cried, holding up what she had found.

"A sash!" Sallie exclaimed.

"It's the sash to that dress we found in the farmhouse," Mandie explained to the others.

"I wonder how it got here," Joe said, looking around the edge of the water.

"I wonder where the dress is," Sallie said.

"Someone probably put it on and wore it," Dimar ventured.

"And lost the sash," Celia added. "How could anyone lose a sash and not know it?"

"That would be easy if it came untied and you didn't

know." Mandie held Snowball tightly with one hand while she put the sash in her apron pocket.

Joe looked puzzled. "I wonder why your Uncle John didn't mention this tunnel."

"He said he hadn't been in the mine—that it was closed when he was a child, and he hired those men to open it. So he wouldn't have known it was here," Mandie replied.

"But the workmen would," Dimar surmised.

"And they would have thought Mr. Shaw knew it was there," Joe reasoned.

"Yes," Hilda agreed.

Surprised, everyone turned to look at her. The girl smiled and hung her head as she clung to Dimar's hand.

"Hilda, you are improving all the time," Mandie told her.

"That is because I am teaching her," Dimar said with a smile.

"Then you'd better keep on teaching her," Joe stated.

"I plan to," Dimar replied.

"Whew! I'm starving!" Celia announced. "And I ate a big meal at noon."

"Me too," Mandie said, heading back toward the tunnel. "Let's go to the house and get something to eat. It must be time for tea by now."

"Are we going back through that tunnel?" Celia asked.

"Sure. We came through it all right, didn't we?" Mandie walked to the entrance.

Joe pointed to his left. "Look! There's a pile of timbers behind those bushes over there."

The others stopped to look.

Dimar examined the boards. "It does not look like new wood," he remarked.

"No, it's probably been here a long time," Mandie agreed.

"All right. Is everybody ready?" Joe lighted the lantern again to go back through the tunnel, and Dimar did the same.

Back inside the mine, Mandie stooped to pick up a handful of gravel and let it trickle through her fingers. "As soon as Uncle John shows us how to do it, we'll begin looking for rubies," she said. "It's hard to believe that such beautiful gems hide in dirt like this."

Her friends all stooped to examine the gravel beneath their feet.

"But that is where they come from," Dimar said. "This man who wants to buy the mine from your uncle must think there are rubies in this mine."

"Yes, I suppose he does, but I don't know anything about him. I think when he was a boy he used to work here with his father," Mandie replied.

"I've been thinking about that, too, Mandie," Joe said, running his fingers through the dirt. "That man must know something about this mine. He must think that it's valuable in some way, or he wouldn't be wanting to put out good money to buy it."

"I know, but Uncle John hasn't told me anything about his dealings with him," Mandie replied.

"He might have already been here and found some rubies," Sallie suggested.

"I don't see how he could. It has been boarded up all these years," Mandie replied.

"It is easy to tear down boards," said Dimar.

"Oh, you're all making it a big mystery," Celia said,

sounding a little frightened. "Maybe there's nothing to it."

"Does the man live near here?" Sallie asked.

"I don't know. All I know about him is what I said, that he used to work here when he was real young. Maybe he just wants the land to build on or something," Mandie said.

"I do not think anyone would want to build on top of land that might have rubies in it," stated Dimar, "but I am sure Mandie's uncle knows what he is doing."

"You're right, Dimar," Celia agreed. "All I know right now is that I'm hungry."

"Me too," said Joe. "Let's go." As he led the way up the steps with the lantern, the others followed, and they raced back to the house on their ponies. Dimar, even though he was leading Hilda's pony, won the race, and Hilda seemed to enjoy the wild ride. Dimar grinned at the others as they caught up with him and Hilda at the gate to the Shaws' house.

"Dimar, we promised we would behave," Mandie reminded him. "It's a wonder Hilda didn't fall off her pony, you were going so fast."

Dimar gently helped Hilda down. "It was not so bad. I am teaching her to ride like a Cherokee."

"Come on. Let's find the food," Joe said, heading up the long walkway to the front door.

Liza, hearing them approaching, opened the door and waited for them.

"De tea, it be ready," she told them. "Did y'all find any rubies?"

"No, Liza, we didn't even look. Uncle John has to show us how," Mandie replied. "None of the grownups are here. Let's have tea in the sun-room."

"All you has to do is dig in de dirt, and I'm sho' you

knows how to dig in de dirt," Liza insisted, following them to the sun-room.

Mandie thought for a moment and said, "I guess you're right, Liza. If the rubies are in the dirt, all we have to do is dig."

Aunt Lou appeared at the doorway. "Liza, come here, git dis food," she called.

Liza obeyed and came back with two large platters loaded with sweetcakes and other goodies. Setting it in the middle of the tea table, she went out and returned with the steaming teapot and cups and saucers.

The Negro girl stood back and surveyed the table as the young people poured the tea and quickly cleaned off the platters. "If dat ain't 'nuff to eat, I can git Jenny to send in mo'," Liza teased.

Everyone laughed.

"I think we'll be doing good to eat all this, Liza," Mandie said. "After all, we have to save room for supper."

"It certainly is a lot of food," Sallie agreed.

"Dat's whut comes from bein' de richest man dis side o' Richmond. It means you kin have anything you wants to eat," Liza said, dancing out of the room.

Everyone looked at each other and laughed.

"Let's go back to the mine after we eat and see if we can find some rubies in that dirt," Celia suggested. "Like Liza said, all we have to do is dig."

"All right," Mandie agreed. "Whoever that dress belongs to might show up, too, looking for the sash." She patted her apron pocket where she had put it.

"I refuse to get involved in another one of your adventures, Mandie," Joe said. "I'll go back to the mine but only to look for rubies."

"Well, that's what we're all going for," Mandie insisted.

As soon as all the food was gone, the group rode back to the mine. They decided to enter by way of the tunnel they had found on their last trip. Riding around to the river side of the tunnel, they dismounted and looked for the entrance. They found it, but it was all boarded up.

"Now, how could that be?" Joe asked, exasperated. He beat on the timbers nailed over the tunnel entrance.

"I don't see how anyone could have closed that up so fast," Mandie said.

"And who would do such a thing?" Sallie asked.

"Maybe it was the person that dress belonged to," Mandie answered.

"Mandie! Stop that!" Joe sputtered. "That dress was in the farmhouse and not in this mine."

"But we found the sash here, remember?" Celia defended her friend.

"Well, anyway, we'll have to go around to the other entrance to get inside the mine unless we want to tear all this down," Joe decided.

"We have no tools for that," Dimar reminded him.

"You're right, Dimar. We'll go around to the front."

Riding around to the other entrance, they tied up their ponies, lighted the two lanterns and descended into the mine.

After the boys used the tools to loosen the dirt, they all scratched around in it for a long time, but they couldn't find anything that they thought might be rubies.

Tired and dirty, they returned to the house just in time to get cleaned up for supper. The adults had already come back.

Mandie related the day's events at the table. "Uncle John, did you know there was a tunnel in the mine that comes out by Rose Creek?" she asked.

"Why, no, I don't know anything about a tunnel," Uncle John replied.

Mandie related how they found the tunnel in the first place and then later found it all boarded up.

"Evidently someone else knows about it, too, if it was open to begin with and then closed when they returned," Dr. Woodard remarked.

Uncle John turned to Uncle Ned. "Do you know anything about this?" he asked.

"Sad, bad mine," the old Indian grunted. Then he went right on eating.

"Uncle Ned, I wish you would tell us whatever you know about the mine," Uncle John told him.

"Put memory away," Uncle Ned insisted.

Uncle John sighed and turned to Mrs. Taft. "You were living here in Franklin when I was a boy. Did you ever know anything about this mine?"

Mrs. Taft cleared her throat. "Nothing that I can think of, John." She, too, went right on eating.

"I don't know what to think," Uncle John said to Dr. Woodard.

"I don't either," the doctor replied, "but I suppose the important thing is to get these young people started on their gem hunting and get it over with."

"You're right," Uncle John agreed. Turning to the young people, he said, "Tomorrow morning we'll take you to the mine and get you started on this mining expedition."

Excited, the young people all spoke at once.

"But you are to be on constant watch for any strangers. Do you all understand that?" Uncle John asked.

"Yes, sir," they chorused.

"John," Elizabeth said quickly, "do you think they'll

be safe there without any adults? With all these strange happenings, I'm not sure we should allow them to stay there without an adult present."

"Well, since there are six of them, I imagine there is safety in numbers." John winked at the young people. "I know I'd hate to come up against the lot of them."

"I still don't know," Elizabeth said uncertainly.

Chapter 5 / The Woman with the Dress

"Now this is how you go about it," Uncle John told the young people as they stood about in the ruby mine the next morning. "You have to get this pump going, like this, in order to get water into the trough." He pumped the handle up and down, flooding the trough with water.

"Will the water stay in the trough?" Mandie asked, watching closely.

"For a while. It slowly runs out the end down there." Uncle John pointed. "But it will stay long enough for you to get a sieveful of gravel washed. Then, if you pump like this, you will notice that the water flows back through the trough. In other words, you are reusing part of the water. Part of it is lost into that trench over there, which becomes a stream as you fill it with water, and then it will flow out to Rose Creek and into the river."

Uncle Ned stood by, silently disapproving of the whole operation.

Dr. Woodard watched. "And you must not pump too fast or the trough will overflow, and you'll get all wet," he reminded them.

"What about the gravel? Won't the trough get full of

gravel when we wash a lot of it?" Joe asked.

"No, not if you do it right," Uncle John replied. "You see, you fill the sieve only partially full of gravel, like this, and dip it into the water without turning it sideways so you won't tilt the gravel out into the trough. The water comes up into the sieve through the bottom and washes the gravel. The tiny particles that are small enough to go through the wire in the bottom of the sieve will go on into the water. But those aren't important. They will all wash away. If you find any rubies, they will be in larger pieces."

"Joe, dig some gravel to put in the sieve," Dr. Woodard told his son.

Joe took the shovel and loosened some dirt and gravel as the others watched.

Uncle John held out the sieve. "Now put enough in this sieve to fill it about half full," he instructed.

Joe did as he was told.

Uncle John turned back to the water trough with the sieve and lowered it straight down into the water without tilting it. The water washed over the gravel, and the tiny particles floated away. He shook the sieve and then set it on the edge of the trough. Running his fingers through the washed gravel, he stirred it around.

The young people watched breathlessly.

"Any rubies?" Celia asked.

"I'm afraid not. It's all rock," Uncle John replied, looking closely at what was left. Then he straightened up. "That's all there is to it," he said.

"But what do we do with what's left in the sieve?" Mandie asked.

"Oh, that. You just dump it over there somewhere away from wherever you want to dig. Otherwise, you'll be digging up the same gravel again," he explained.

"This is going to be a very interesting experience," Dimar remarked. "Perhaps I will find a ruby."

"Remember to look at everything very closely," Dr. Woodard cautioned. "I've told you what a ruby should look like. It will be dark and rough, and you could easily mistake it for an ordinary rock," he said.

"Are we staying all day?" Celia asked.

"No, you must come home to eat at noon. That way we'll know you are all right," Uncle John replied.

"But we can come back here after we eat, can't we?" Mandie asked.

"I suppose so—if you're not too tired after all the work you're going to do," Uncle John teased. "Whoever does the digging is going to be worn out."

"We can all do our own digging. There are enough tools over there for all of us," Mandie decided.

Uncle John took a step backward. "Dr. Woodard, Uncle Ned, and I have somewhere we have to go," he informed them. "We're going to leave you here, so please be careful. Don't get too close to each other when you're digging or someone could be hit," he warned. "I'm depending on you all to act like the intelligent young people I know you to be."

"Thank you, Mr. Shaw," said Dimar.

"We will be careful," Sallie assured him.

As the men started to leave, Uncle Ned took Mandie's hand. "Papoose, be careful," he cautioned.

"I will, Uncle Ned," Mandie promised. Then turning to Uncle John, she said, "We'll bring home all the rubies we find." She laughed.

Uncle John winked. "Yes, you be sure to do that."

As the men left, the young people made a dash for the tools.

"I think I'll use a hoe," Mandie stated, taking a long-handled one. "It might be easier to handle than a pick."

The others chose various hoes, shovels, and picks and scattered about in the mine, beginning their task.

Dimar took Hilda over to the far side and showed her how to use a hoe. "Dig. Like this," he explained, digging into the dirt.

Hilda watched and then took the hoe to imitate him. She laughed and kept digging away.

Dimar moved away from her for fear of being hit and began his own search.

They all rushed to see who could get a sieve of gravel to wash first. Uncle John had provided sieves for each of them, and there was a lot of splashing and excitement as they washed the gravel and searched for something that might look like a ruby.

"Oh! Is this one?" Celia cried, holding up a dark-colored rock she had washed.

The others crowded close to examine it.

"It looks like just an old rock to me," Mandie said.

"Yeah, it's just a rock," Joe agreed.

"Oh well, there are lots more," Celia said, dumping the contents of her sieve in the pile of discarded gravel in the corner.

"Yes, there are more than we can ever sift through," Sallie remarked as she continued digging.

"I wish it was summertime and school was out, so we could have more time. We might find something then," said Mandie.

"But your Uncle John will be selling the mine by then," Celia reminded her.

"Yes, and that other man may be getting a rich mine. We will never know because we do not have time to do much," Dimar said as he looked over at Hilda digging away in the corner.

"Hey, less talk and more work, or we'll never get done," Joe called loudly.

"Joe is right. We must concentrate on what we are doing, or we may overlook a ruby," Sallie agreed, bending to fill her sieve.

Hilda stopped digging and stooped to examine the gravel, jabbering incoherently.

Everyone looked over at her.

"What is it, Hilda?" Mandie asked, hurrying to her side.

Hilda pointed to what looked like a piece of broken pottery sticking out of the ground. Mandie bent to pick it up, but Hilda snatched it and quickly put it in her apron pocket. When the others crowded around, Hilda kept her hand tightly over her pocket and backed away.

"What is it, Mandie?" Celia asked.

"It looked like a piece of broken pottery, but it was so dirty I'm not sure," Mandie replied.

"Hilda, will you let us see what you found?" Dimar asked, approaching her cautiously.

Hilda backed away quickly and kept her hand over her pocket.

"It's all right, Hilda. Go ahead and dig. You may find something else," Mandie told the girl.

As the others went back to their digging, Hilda finally picked up her hoe and moved over to a corner by herself to resume digging.

"Well, at least someone found something," Joe said.

The morning slipped away rapidly, and no one else found anything. But the girls' aprons had become very soiled, and everyone's shoes were full of dirt.

"Whew!" Mandie said, standing on one foot to empty

the dirt out of her shoe. "It must be time to go eat."

"Not tired, are you?" Joe asked, pausing to wipe a dirty hand across his face.

"Not until I stop," Mandie said. "As long as I am digging, I don't think about being tired."

Celia tried to shake the dirt off her apron. "I sure need a bath," she said.

"Do you think we can get cleaned up enough to be allowed to sit at the table and eat?" Sallie laughed.

"I think so," Mandie replied.

"Maybe this afternoon we will find a ruby," Dimar remarked. "Maybe we will find several rubies."

"Yes," Hilda spoke up.

When they returned for the noon meal, Elizabeth met them at the door and quickly looked them over. "I suppose you're not as dirty as I thought you would be," she said. "Get washed now and get to the table."

"Oh, what fun it was, Mother!" Mandie exclaimed as the young people filed into the hallway.

"But no rubies yet," Joe added.

"Of course not." Uncle John spoke up from the doorway to the parlor. "You couldn't have that much luck," he laughed.

"Hilda did find something," Celia said, turning to the girl who was hovering at the edge of the group. "Where is that thing you found, Hilda?"

Hilda backed off, keeping her hand on the pocket of her apron.

"I think it was only a piece of a broken bowl," Mandie said.

"All right. Get washed, all of you—and hurry," Elizabeth told them.

As they scampered in different directions to wash,

Mandie took charge of Hilda. "Come on, Hilda. We've got to wash so we can eat," she said.

When they all returned to the dining room, the young people ate as though they were starved to death. The morning's exercise had whetted their appetites.

Mrs. Taft stopped eating and watched them. "You all must be in a big hurry to get back to that digging," she said.

"Oh, yes, Grandmother," Mandie replied.

Hilda shook her head violently.

Dimar spoke to her gently. "Do you not want to go back to the mine and dig with us?" he asked.

Hilda shook her head again.

Grandmother Taft smiled at Hilda. "That's all right," she said. "She can stay here with us older folks this time."

Mandie wondered why Hilda suddenly didn't want to go back, but she also felt a little relieved. "Are you going this afternoon, Uncle Ned?" she asked the Indian, who had been silent during the meal.

"Not today. Later," he replied.

"We have guests coming this afternoon," Uncle John explained, "and we want Uncle Ned to meet them."

"That's all right. We'll be fine," Mandie assured the old Indian. But she continued watching him. He seemed to be in bad spirits and wasn't joining in the conversation. Actually, Grandmother Taft acted as though she had a secret, too. Perhaps they were involved in some kind of conspiracy. Mandie was anxious to find out what it was.

Elizabeth looked around the table and saw that all the young people had finished eating. "You may go now," she said. "But please be careful."

"And remember. You must all be back here before the sun goes down," Mrs. Woodard reminded them.

The young people scrambled to their feet.

"I wish you could go, Uncle Ned," Mandie urged, stopping by his chair as she left the room.

"Later, Papoose. I promise," Uncle Ned said, squeezing her hand. "If Papoose get in trouble, I will go."

Mandie didn't understand what he meant, but since the others were leaving, she released Uncle Ned's wrinkled hand and hurried from the room.

As they guided their ponies back toward the mine, Mandie called to the others, "Let's go down by the river first and see if that tunnel is still closed."

"I was going to suggest the same thing," Joe called back.

They carefully made their way through the underbrush toward Rose Creek. As they came within sight of the end of the tunnel, they were amazed to see a man and a woman, carrying heavy bags, get into a boat.

"The dress! That woman is wearing that dress!" Mandie cried as she raced her pony forward. She squinted but she couldn't see their faces. By the time the young people got to the creek bank, the man and woman had rowed far out into the water.

Mandie put her hands on her hips. "Of all things! Get this close and still not close enough!"

"They probably are carrying gems from your uncle's mine in those bags," said Dimar.

Joe laughed. "In those bags? We dug all morning and couldn't find a single stone, and you think they had bags full of them?"

"Of course. That is why we cannot find any. They got them all," Dimar replied.

Joe laughed again.

"I wonder who they are," Sallie said as the boat moved

out of sight around a bend. "Do you suppose the dress belongs to that woman or do you think she just found it in the farmhouse and put it on?"

"I sure would like to know. I still have the sash," Mandie said, patting her apron pocket.

"Now we do have a mystery, don't we?" Celia said.

"And as far as I'm concerned, it's going to remain an unsolved mystery," Joe declared. "Come on. Let's get busy."

The entrance to the tunnel was still closed, so Joe led the way around to the front entrance of the mine. There they tied up their ponies and went down into the mine to continue their work.

Although they worked hard that afternoon, digging and sifting gravel, they didn't find a single interesting thing. They checked the tunnel entrance several times to be sure the man and woman had not returned, but there was no sign of them.

The young people got home in plenty of time to bathe and change clothes before sundown.

As they all sat down to supper, Mandie could hardly wait to share her news about the strangers. "Uncle John, we saw a woman wearing that dress we found in your old house," she began excitedly. "And there was a man with her. They got into a boat down by the end of the tunnel and disappeared."

Elizabeth put down her fork. "What!" she exclaimed.

"You saw a woman wearing the dress you found?" Uncle John questioned her. "What did she look like?"

"We couldn't get close enough to tell. They were carrying some heavy bags. And the back entrance to the tunnel is still closed."

"Seems like some shenanigans are going on down

at that mine," Dr. Woodard said.

Uncle Ned and Mrs. Taft leaned forward to listen.

Elizabeth looked worried. "Strangers at the mine? John, what is going on?" she asked.

"I don't know, dear," he replied. "Something strange for sure." Turning back to the young people, he asked, "Did none of you get close enough to see who they were, or what they looked like?"

There was a chorus of nos as the young people shook their heads.

"You'd better not go back to that mine again unless an adult is with you," Elizabeth instructed. "We don't know who these people are."

"Why get worried over a couple of strangers, Elizabeth?" Mrs. Taft asked. "There are strangers everywhere that we don't know."

"Elizabeth is right," John said. "It will be safer if they don't go back unless one of us is with them. That place is more or less isolated."

Mandie turned to Uncle Ned, who had not said a word. "Uncle Ned, will you go with us tomorrow? Please?" Mandie begged.

The old Indian shook his head. "Sad, bad mine. Better Papoose not go."

She looked at her uncle. "Uncle John, please go with us so we can go back tomorrow."

"I can't tomorrow morning. I have something else to do. Maybe I can tomorrow afternoon," he said.

"I am beginning to wonder if you should go back there at all, even with someone with you," Mrs. Woodard cautioned. "We don't know who those people are."

"I think it will be safe if we go with them," Dr. Woodard replied.

"We'll be back before noon tomorrow, Mandie, and we'll go to the mine right after we eat," Uncle John promised.

Mandie sighed. "Well, then, I suppose we'll have to wait until tomorrow afternoon," she said, not realizing what lay ahead.

Chapter 6 / Mandie and Joe in Trouble

The next morning was cool and cloudy, and when Mandie, Celia, and Sallie awoke, Hilda wasn't in her bed. Dressing quickly, the three girls ran down to Liza's room to see if Hilda was there. But Liza was already up, helping in the kitchen. There was no sign of Hilda.

"Liza, did Hilda sleep in your room last night?" Mandie asked as the girls entered the kitchen.

"Not so's I'd notice," Liza replied. "Is dat girl missin' agin?"

"Yes," said Sallie. "Do you know where she might be?"

"Dat girl might be anywheres," Liza answered with a sigh. "Guess we better start huntin'."

"Huntin' for what?" asked Joe as he and Dimar joined the girls in the kitchen."

"For Hilda," Mandie replied.

"She's missing again," Celia added.

Joe shook his head. "I know you care a lot about her, Mandie, but sometimes . . ."

"I know what you mean," Mandie admitted.

"We should look for her in the house first," Dimar suggested.

"Right," said Joe. "The five of us could search the whole house in a short time if we split up."

In less than a half hour, the five young people had searched all three floors of the house, the secret tunnel, the stables, and everywhere else they could think of. But there was no sign of Hilda anywhere.

When they started questioning the servants, the servants all said they hadn't seen her since the night before—all except Jason Bond. He remembered seeing her very early that morning standing out by the gate.

"What was she doing out there?" Dimar asked.

"Just starin' into space," the caretaker responded. "That's all."

The men had already left for the morning, so when the young people told Elizabeth about Hilda's disappearance, she called the servants together and asked for their help in finding the girl.

"Oh, I feel so responsible," said Mrs. Taft after the servants left on their search. "Maybe I shouldn't have brought her here."

"Nonsense, Mother," Elizabeth replied. "The servants will check with all the neighbors and some of our friends in town, and I even asked Jason Bond to see if she might have tried to find her way back to the mine."

"I do not think she would be there," Dimar offered.

"Dimar's right," Mandie agreed. "I don't think she liked that place. She wouldn't go back with us yesterday."

"Perhaps not," Elizabeth said, "but we must look everywhere. Why don't you young people search the house and grounds again. Maybe she's hiding somewhere."

"Hilda's good at hiding, isn't she, Mandie?" Celia laughed.

"Yes, she sure is," Mandie nodded. "She was hiding in that attic at school a long time before we found her. Come on, everybody," she said to her friends, "let's stay together this time and search real good. We've got to find her before Uncle John gets back."

But after another long, careful search, they still couldn't find Hilda or any clue to where she might be. About mid-morning they joined Elizabeth and Mrs. Taft and Mrs. Woodard in the parlor.

"No success?" asked Grandmother Taft.

The young people shook their heads silently.

Just then Liza rushed into the parlor, out of breath. "'Scuse me, Miz Shaw," she said, panting. "We done found her, but she won't come. I'se sorry, ma'am. I don't know what's wrong wid her."

"Found her where?" Elizabeth asked.

"Over t' the Hadleys, Miz Shaw," Liza replied.

"Way over there?" Elizabeth exclaimed.

"I'll go get her, Mother," Mandie offered. "She'll come back for me."

"But you don't know where the Hadleys live, dear," Elizabeth said.

"I do, Mrs. Shaw," Joe spoke up. "I've been there on calls with my father. I'll go after her."

"She doesn't know you very well, Joe, but she would come for me. Mrs. Woodard, couldn't Joe go with me to get her?" Mandie asked.

"Of course, dear," Mrs. Woodard replied. "You mustn't go by yourself."

Elizabeth looked relieved. "You may go if you promise to go straight there and back," she agreed. "And if she won't come back with you, you are to return immediately. We'll figure out some other way to get her."

"Yes, Mother," said Mandie. "I promise."

Elizabeth turned to Joe. "Now, Joe, please be careful. Hilda is so unpredictable, and I'm counting on you to keep Amanda out of trouble."

"I will," Joe agreed.

Instantly the other young people clamored to go along.

"No, no," Elizabeth told them. "It will be easier for them to handle Hilda if you all will stay here."

The others reluctantly agreed.

Elizabeth gave her daughter a hug. "Now you two get on out to the stable. Jason Bond took the rig out looking for Hilda, and he isn't back yet, so you can ride your ponies," Elizabeth explained. "And remember, straight there and back, no loitering along the way. Now make haste."

"Yes, ma'am," Mandie replied, picking up Snowball.

"Yes, ma'am," Joe echoed.

Within minutes Mandie and Joe were headed in the direction of the Hadleys' house with Snowball clinging to Mandie's shoulder.

"I don't know why you had to bring that cat," Joe grumbled.

"Snowball needs some outdoor air," Mandie defended herself. "Besides, Hilda is fascinated by him. I may be able to entice her to leave by letting her hold him."

"I hope we can get her to come back," said Joe.

"Where do the Hadleys live?" Mandie asked.

"Not too far," he answered, "but we have to go near the mine."

Mandie perked up. "We do?"

"The road goes pretty close," Joe said as they trotted on.

"Do you think we could just go down the road that runs by the mine on our way to the Hadleys?" Mandie asked.

"What for?"

"Just to look at it as we go by," she said. "If we're going to be that close to it, I don't see why we can't just ride by and look."

Joe thought for a moment. "Well, all right," he agreed. "But remember, we will not stop, no matter what excuse you think up," he stated.

Mandie smiled. "Thanks, Joe," she said as the wind blew her bonnet back from her long blonde hair.

At a fork in the road Joe turned left and Mandie followed. She soon recognized the road as the one they had traveled to the mine from a different direction.

As they came within sight of the mine, Mandie suddenly pulled up the reins on her pony. "Look, Joe! There are two horses tied over there in the trees," she called to him.

Joe slowed his pony to a leisurely walk. "I wonder who they belong to," he said.

They both stopped in the road near the mine, and Mandie stayed at Joe's side. "We could just go down there long enough to see who's there," she suggested.

"You promised your mother you wouldn't go anywhere except straight to the Hadleys and back, remember?" Joe reminded her.

"Well, it wouldn't hurt anything if we just looked to see who it is," Mandie argued.

"But there's no one in sight. Someone must have just left the horses there for some reason," Joe objected.

Suddenly they heard the sound of hammering coming from the mine, and then the noise of planks being moved around. The two looked at each other in alarm.

"Joe?" Mandie gripped Snowball with one hand and slid down from her pony.

"Just remember, you started this," he said, dismounting.

"All right, I'm guilty," Mandie admitted.

They quickly tied their ponies out of sight and then softly made their way toward the mine. Stopping behind two huge tree trunks, they watched the entrance to the mine as Snowball clung silently to the shoulder of Mandie's dress.

Then the noise stopped.

The two were so intent upon watching the entrance of the mine that they didn't see or hear anyone behind them.

Suddenly two pairs of strong hands grabbed them.

Mandie gasped and looked up into the face of an old woman. Joe swung around just as a big, burly man threw a rope around him, tying his arms and hands.

Mandie trembled with fear. "Who are you? What do you want?" she managed to ask as she held Snowball tightly.

Then all of a sudden she realized that the woman was wearing the blue gingham dress. And there on the ground by the strangers' feet lay two big, heavy canvas bags.

"I know where you got that dress," Mandie told the old woman. "I saw it in the farmhouse over there on the other side of the trees. What was it doing there? Did you steal it?"

The old woman grabbed Mandie's hand and gave it a hard jerk. Mandie winced with pain.

"Ain't none of your business," the old woman said.

Joe tried to free himself but the huge man was too

strong for him. "Let me go!" Joe demanded.

"Why? So you can go spread the word that we've been here? Never!" the man replied, holding tightly to the rope.

"What are we agoin' to do with 'em?" the woman asked.

"That depends," the man replied. "Could be a right serious situation, you know."

"Long as they don't know what we's got in them bags we'll be all right," the woman argued.

"What do you have in those bags?" Mandie asked.

"You shore ain't gonna find out," the man said. "Else you could suffer some bad consequences."

"Let me loose," Joe demanded. "Are you going to stand there all day doing nothing? We've got somewhere we've got to go."

"You ain't goin' nowhere, so don't git your dander up," the old man told him. "That is, nowhere without us."

"You mean you're going to take us with you?" Mandie asked.

The old woman looked sharply at her companion. "That ain't necessary, is it?"

"I think so. Jest long enough for us to be on our way," the man said.

Joe tried to free his hands as the man tightened the rope around him. "Where are we going?" he asked.

The man ignored him.

"I suppose you stole whatever is in the bags, and now you're running away," Mandie said.

"Now you listen here, you young squirt," the old man said angrily. "What's in them bags ain't none of your business, and you'd better shet up about it, or you'll wish you had."

"Let's git on our way. I don't care whether we take

these two or not, but I want to git goin'," the woman said.

"All right, we'll go. I'll hold on to the girl while you untie the horses and shoo them off. We'll take the boat." The man reached for Mandie's hand and gripped it in his big fist.

"What'll we do when we git back. The horses'll be gone," the woman protested.

"Don't worry 'bout them horses. We'll find a way," the man said. "Now hurry up and do what I told you to."

The old woman hurried over to the two horses, untied them, and slapped them with the reins. The horses neighed and took off running through the woods.

Mandie held her breath, hoping the ponies, which were tethered out of sight, wouldn't make a sound to call attention to themselves.

The woman came back and grabbed Mandie's hand again, and the man pushed Joe forward.

"Into the mine," the old man ordered.

The woman pushed and pulled Mandie along with her, and Snowball dug his claws into Mandie's shoulder.

"Are you leavin' the bags?" the woman asked her partner.

"Nope. I'll git 'em soon as I tie these two up," he said.

The strangers marched the young people through the mine and the tunnel, and on to Rose Creek where there was a boat tied up.

"You'll get in trouble for doing this," Mandie told them.

"And it'll be big trouble. Don't you know who she is?" Joe asked, nodding to Mandie.

"Don't make no difference," the man said.

"It does, too. She is John Shaw's niece, and he owns

this mine!" Joe yelled as the old man shoved him toward a tree.

The woman brought Mandie near, and the man quickly wrapped the rope around the two, pinning them to the tree.

"I said it don't make no difference who she is," the old man repeated. He turned to the woman. "You watch 'em so they can't git loose," he commanded. "I'll git the bags."

The woman did as she was told, and the man hurried back through the tunnel.

"Don't you see you're making unnecessary trouble for yourself?" Mandie asked the woman. "We were on the way to the Hadleys, and if you'll just let us loose, we'll go on our way."

"That's easier said than done," the old woman said.

"And we won't even tell anyone that we saw you," Joe added.

"He's the boss," the old woman said.

"But if you do what he says, you'll be in trouble, too," Mandie told her.

"That's right. They call that a conspiracy, I think. They can arrest you for being an accessory to the fact," Joe told her.

The woman just looked at him, not understanding what he was talking about.

"Who are you, anyway?" Mandie asked. "And where are you going with those bags?"

"I ain't tellin' you no more. Them bags ain't none of your business," the woman replied. "Now shet up about it." She slapped Mandie on the cheek, leaving a red hand-print.

Tears filled Mandie's eyes at the pain, but she tried to keep calm.

"Stop that!" Joe scolded the woman. "Don't do that anymore, or I'll see that you pay for it."

"You ain't the boss," the woman said. "He is." She nodded at the man emerging from the tunnel, carrying the two heavy bags. He threw the bags into the boat.

"That woman slapped Mandie for no reason at all, and I don't like it," Joe protested.

The man glanced at Mandie and then at his companion. "Behave yourself, woman!" he snapped. "I'm in charge of this."

The woman looked away.

"Now hold on to that girl," he ordered. "I'm goin' to untie them so we can git them into the boat." He turned to untie the knots.

As the rope came loose, the woman grabbed Mandie's hand.

The man shoved Joe, still partly tied up, toward the boat. "Git in!" he shouted.

"Where are we going?" Joe demanded.

"I said git in that boat," the man repeated, giving the boy a shove. Joe stumbled and almost fell head over heels into the boat.

Mandie's heart raced as she realized they were being taken away somewhere down the river. She had to leave some kind of a clue. Quickly putting Snowball on her shoulder, she reached surreptitiously into her apron pocket, pulled out the light blue sash she had found, and dropped it behind her as the woman shoved her forward.

The man rowed the boat out into deeper water. "You can untie the ropes now. I don't think they'll try to jump overboard and swim from here."

"I can't swim anyway," Mandie informed him.

"That's good. If your friend can swim, he wouldn't try to git away without you, I'm sure." He laughed.

The man rowed farther and farther down Rose Creek toward the wide open Little Tennessee River. The sky was still cloudy and a light fog started forming over the water.

Mandie looked at her captors, feeling a mixture of fear and anger. "I'm sure you have stolen something out of our mine, haven't you?"

"Ain't nothin' in these here bags out of your mine," the man argued.

"But you're stealing something," Mandie said angrily. "You're still breaking one of the Ten Commandments—'Thou shalt not steal!'—and that is a terrible thing to do."

"Listen, miss, mind your own business," the man replied.

Then the woman spoke up. "We ain't the only ones that's been stealin'," she said.

"I knew you had stolen something," Mandie declared.

"Woman, shet your mouth!" the man yelled.

"You've made one good step. You've admitted your sin, that you have stolen something," Mandie said shakily. "But you must ask forgiveness from God and try to make amends for what you've done."

The woman stared at her in silence, but the man just ignored Mandie.

"What you steal will never do you any good," Joe put in.

"No, it won't, because it will bother your conscience," Mandie told the woman, feeling a little more bold. "I will help you pray for forgiveness if you want me to."

"I don't need no forgiveness for nothin'," the woman muttered.

"Yes, you do. You need our forgiveness for what you're doing to us," Mandie said. "It's a sin to hold things against people when they do you wrong. You might not exactly like what they do to you, but Christians have to forgive other people." Mandie swallowed hard. "I forgive y'all for what you've done to us. Won't you ask God to forgive you?"

With Snowball curled up in her lap, Mandie fearfully reached across to the woman and put her small hand over an old wrinkled one. She searched the woman's tired eyes.

The woman quickly pulled her hand away and wouldn't look at Mandie.

"Your daddy a preacher or somethin'?" the old man asked.

"No, my daddy is in heaven with God," Mandie said sadly, "but he was a good man. He taught me that God loves us and will forgive us for our sins if we'll tell Him we're sorry."

The woman just stared at Mandie again.

"If you think you can persuade us to let you go with that kind of talk, you might as well shet up because it won't work," the old man said. "If there's a God up there, He shore has forsaken us. I done give up on that stuff a long time ago."

As they traveled downstream, Joe looked all around. "Where are we going?" he ventured to ask. His voice was a little shaky.

"That I ain't tellin' neither," the man said.

"I reckon I'll see when we get there then," Joe replied.

The man pulled hard on the oars as they swept

through a strong current. "We may not be goin' to the same place," he said.

Mandie and Joe glanced at each other. What were these people up to, anyway? And how would anyone ever find them? No one could track them in the water. Was there no way to get to these people's hearts?

Mandie tried again. "Do y'all have any children?"

The old woman shook her head while the man ignored the question.

"I am my mother's only child," Mandie said. "She loves me an awful lot, and I love her more than anything. She's going to be worried about me when I don't get back home on time," Mandie said. "You see, my grandmother didn't like my father because he was half Cherokee. After I was born, she made my father take me and leave. I wasn't reunited with my mother until after my father died. You see, his old Indian friend, Uncle Ned, helped me get to my Uncle John Shaw's house in Frank—"

"Shet up!" the man shouted. "What's all that got to do with us?"

"Maybe you didn't catch what Mandie said," Joe answered bravely. "She is part Cherokee, and the Cherokees will come looking for her when she doesn't show up back at the house. I'd sure hate to come up against those Indians when one of their kin has been wronged."

"Indians?" the woman echoed.

"That's what he said," the man told her. "Don't you remember all that hullabaloo about the Indians and that mine?"

"I suppose so. Seems like I remember somethin'," the woman said.

Mandie and Joe exchanged glances.

"What about the Indians and that mine?" Mandie asked.

"Nothin' you need to know," the man said.

"I *am* part Cherokee," Mandie admitted," "but I wouldn't ask the Cherokees to harm you in any way. Most of my Cherokee kinpeople are Christians, and they believe like I do, that we must forgive each other. They wouldn't carry off any white children for no reason at all. They know God sees and hears everything, and they want to live by His Word. But if you harm us, they will see that you are punished."

The old woman fidgeted with her blue gingham dress. "Maybe we's doin' somethin' we shouldn't—"

"Keep your trap shet, woman!" the man yelled. "Don't you see what they's tryin' to do? They think they can sweet-talk us into lettin' 'em go, and then they'll go straight to John Shaw with a tale and—"

"We wouldn't cause you any trouble, mister," Mandie interrupted. "Just let us go home. My mother must be awfully worried by now."

Suddenly the man turned the boat toward the creek bank. Mandie's heart leaped in anticipation. Maybe he was going to set them free.

"Grab a bag, woman," the man ordered as he brought the boat near the bank.

Mandie and Joe silently looked at each other. Could they make a run for it? But the man quickly threw the bags on the bank as the woman jumped out onto the sand. Then the man gave the boat a sharp push with the oars as he jumped out, taking the oars with him.

Joe tried to jump out, but the man hit him hard with an oar, knocking him down into the boat.

Mandie held Snowball tightly as the boat rocked and swirled about, floating swiftly down Rose Creek toward the river. She bent over Joe. He looked lifeless. "Joe! Joe!

Wake up!" she cried, tears streaming down her pale cheeks.

Fearfully, she watched the man and woman pick up their bags and hurry off into the woods without looking back. "Help us, please," Mandie yelled. "Joe is hurt!"

Pushing Joe's hair back from his forehead, she gently touched his cheek. Then she took his limp hands in hers and rubbed them. He didn't move or open his eyes.

As the boat drifted free in the swift current, Mandie sat up on the seat. Gripping Snowball with one hand, she held on to the side of the boat and looked toward the sky. The sun had come out. "Dear God, please help us!" she prayed. "Please! Please don't let Joe die!"

Snowball meowed, protesting the tight grip she had on him, and Mandie held him up to her face to cuddle him. "Snowball, I love you!" she whispered through her tears. "I didn't mean to squeeze you so hard. It's just that I'm so scared. Joe is hurt and the boat is drifting away. We may all be drowned!"

She took a deep breath and wiped her sleeve across her tear-stained face as the boat bumped and swirled.

"Now that's not the way to act at all," she scolded herself. She looked toward the sky again and began quoting her favorite verse: " 'What time I am afraid I will put my trust in Thee.' Oh, God," she prayed, "I know you'll take care of us, but please hurry!"

Chapter 7 / The Search Begins

When John, Uncle Ned, and Dr. Woodard returned home a little before noon, they found the worried women sitting by the window in the parlor. Elizabeth and Mrs. Woodard told them about Hilda's disappearance and about sending Mandie and Joe to get her.

"But they should have returned long before now," Mrs. Woodard said.

Elizabeth rose from her chair and clutched her husband's arm. "Amanda promised to go straight to the Hadleys and back without stopping anywhere," she told him.

"You know Amanda as well as I do," John said with a smile. "She probably found something interesting on the way."

"But Joe was with her, and I'm sure he would have reminded her that they were to go there and back without any delay," Elizabeth replied.

"We find," Uncle Ned said, putting a hand on Elizabeth's shoulder. "Do not worry. We go to Hadleys now."

"Yes, we'll go right now," Dr. Woodard agreed.

John Shaw put his arm around his wife. "Don't worry, dear. With Uncle Ned's help I'm sure we'll find them."

Elizabeth dabbed at her eyes with her handkerchief. "You know how I love Amanda," she said. "If anything ever happened to her, I'd never get over it."

Mrs. Taft looked up from her needlework. "Elizabeth, you don't give Amanda credit for having any sense. She knows how much she means to you. I'm sure she has just been delayed at the Hadleys. Maybe she couldn't get Hilda to come back with her."

"In that case, they were to come on back without her," Elizabeth replied.

"Come back to your needlework, dear," said Mrs. Taft. "The men will find Amanda and Joe, I am sure."

"That's right," Dr. Woodard said. "We'll find them."

"Where are the other young people?" John asked.

"Probably out in the kitchen worrying Jenny for goodies," Elizabeth said, managing a smile. "But you will go right now, won't you?"

"Yes, dear. We'll leave right now." John kissed his wife on the forehead and started outside with Uncle Ned and Dr. Woodard.

Quickly mounting their horses, the men rode over to the Hadleys. As they approached the huge old house, their eyes quickly searched the grounds for Mandie's and Joe's ponies. There was only one pony at the hitching post, and it was not familiar to them.

"Either they have already come and gone, or they never got here at all," John said.

"I'd say you're right about that," Dr. Woodard agreed.

"We find," Uncle Ned grunted.

They dismounted and walked up to the front door. As John Shaw reached up to use the knocker, the door opened, and there stood Hilda.

The men looked at her in astonishment. Hilda

reached to take Dr. Woodard's hand and tried to lead him back down the walkway.

"Home," she said, smiling.

"Wait," Dr. Woodard told her.

Mrs. Hadley appeared in the doorway with her walking cane. "John, I am so glad to see you," she said. "This poor girl just appeared on our doorstep this morning, and she wouldn't go home when Liza came for her. She has been sitting in the parlor all morning, never saying a word, just smiling at me." The elderly woman looked bewildered.

"I'm sorry, ma'am," John replied. "Elizabeth sent Amanda and Joe after her, but evidently they never got here."

"Why, no. I haven't seen another soul all day," Mrs. Hadley said.

The men exchanged glances.

"We find," Uncle Ned insisted.

"Well, I do hope you find them right away," said Mrs. Hadley. "They mustn't be out too late. The days are getting shorter, you know. It will be dark early."

"Evidently Hilda is in the mood to go home. Why don't I take her back to your house while you and Uncle Ned ride around looking for them?" Dr. Woodard offered.

"That's a good idea," agreed John. "You go ahead with her. Uncle Ned and I will work our way back toward the mine. That's the only place I can imagine they went."

After they bade Mrs. Hadley goodbye, Dr. Woodard helped Hilda onto his horse with him, giving her stern instructions to hang on tightly all the way back to John Shaw's house. Apparently she understood, and they started off down the road.

Uncle Ned and John mounted their horses.

"Two roads go to mine," Uncle Ned stated.

"That's right. There are two ways to get there from here. Why don't you go that way?" John said, indicating the road to the right. "I'll take the other road, and we'll meet at the mine."

Uncle Ned nodded. "We meet," he replied.

The old Indian rode off to the right, carefully watching the road for tracks. John Shaw went the other way.

When Dr. Woodard and Hilda arrived at John Shaw's house, Elizabeth greeted them at the door.

"Amanda and Joe weren't at the Hadleys?" she asked.

"Mrs. Hadley had not seen them," Dr. Woodard told her. "But Hilda came with me readily enough."

Elizabeth put her hand on Hilda's arm to keep her from running off somewhere again. "Hilda, we will find Liza to entertain you awhile," she told the girl. Turning back to Dr. Woodard, she asked. "Where are John and Uncle Ned?"

"They're coming back by the mine. That's the only place we could figure the two might have stopped," Dr. Woodard answered. "If they don't find them there, John or Uncle Ned will come back here to get me to help search."

Elizabeth sighed. "Where, oh where can those two be?"

"I'm afraid only the Lord knows that right now, Elizabeth," Dr. Woodard replied.

"Go on into the dining room. We decided to start eating since we didn't know how long you all would be gone," Elizabeth said. "Come on, Hilda, we will eat and then we will find Liza."

The girl smiled and followed Elizabeth and Dr. Woodard into the dining room. Then spying Dimar, she plopped down in the chair next to him.

Immediately, all the young people at the table bombarded Dr. Woodard with questions.

"Did you find Amanda and Joe?" Mrs. Woodard asked.

Dr. Woodard shook his head.

"Weren't they at the Hadleys?" Celia dabbed her lips with her linen napkin.

The doctor held a chair for Elizabeth, then sat down on the other side of the table. "No, they haven't been there," he answered.

"We have decided that they went to the mine," Dimar volunteered.

"Why is that?" Elizabeth asked.

"Because Mandie is so enthralled by the place, and there is a mystery about it," Dimar replied.

"A mystery?" Elizabeth questioned.

"A mystery about why the mine was closed and why Uncle Ned won't talk about it," Celia put in.

"There is no mystery about that," Mrs. Taft spoke up. "John's father just decided to close the mine years ago, and that's that."

"My grandfather knows something that we do not know about the mine," Sallie said.

"You really believe that, don't you?" returned Mrs. Woodard.

"Yes, we all believe it. There is something he is not telling about the mine, and Mandie would like to find out what it is," Sallie explained.

"Amanda had better get that out of her head because there is no mystery," Mrs. Taft said.

Elizabeth sat forward. "Mother, you know Uncle Ned

has been acting mysterious about the mine. He won't talk about it."

"And he keeps saying it is a sad, bad mine," Sallie added.

"You can remember that far back, Mother," Elizabeth prodded. "What was the reason for closing the mine?"

Mrs. Taft looked around the table. "I have forgotten, dear. That was so long ago. What difference does it make now?"

"I don't know what difference it makes now because I don't know why it was closed," Elizabeth persisted.

Hilda, having listened to the conversation around her, turned to Dimar. "Sad, bad mine!" she exclaimed.

Everyone laughed.

"Hilda has learned to say that, too," Sallie said.

Hilda's face clouded in anger. With tears in her big brown eyes, she banged her fist on the table and yelled, "Do not laugh! Sad, bad mine."

Dimar reached for her hand and spoke softly to her. "Yes, it is a sad, bad mine."

Hilda sighed and picked up her fork to resume eating.

"I think we have said enough for now. Let's eat," Elizabeth said. "We don't want to upset anyone."

"John and Uncle Ned should be along soon," Dr. Woodard remarked. "They've had time to go by the mine."

"I hope they have Amanda and Joe with them," Elizabeth said.

Just then Liza trudged into the dining room and spoke to Elizabeth. "Mistuh Shaw and dat Mistuh Injun man comin' up de road. Got two ponies wid 'em," she informed them.

They all started to leave the table, but Elizabeth

stopped them with a wave of her hand. "Please don't get up," she said. "They will be hungry. They can join us here at the table."

The others sat back down and waited. In a minute John Shaw and Uncle Ned, dejected and tired, entered the room.

"We might as well eat, Uncle Ned," John said, taking a place and indicating one for Uncle Ned. "Well, Elizabeth, Mrs. Woodard, we haven't found them yet. They had been at the mine. Their ponies were tied up near there, but since we couldn't find Joe and Amanda, we brought their ponies home. As soon as we eat a bite, we'll look some more."

Mrs. Woodard took a deep breath and said nothing.

Elizabeth's blue eyes filled with tears. "John, where can they be?" she asked.

"I have no idea. We thought that with Dimar's help, we would spread out from the mine and keep looking," John replied, helping himself to the food on the table in front of him.

"I will be glad to help, Mr. Shaw," Dimar responded.

Elizabeth sighed. "Oh, if only Amanda hadn't disobeyed . . ."

Everyone was silent for a moment.

"Tunnel in mine open," Uncle Ned stated at last.

"It is?" Celia gasped.

"But it was closed with boards when we left!" Sallie exclaimed.

"Do you think Amanda and Joe might have removed the boards?" Dr. Woodard asked.

"They could have if they had had a hammer, but there was no hammer at the mine when we were there, only hoes, shovels, and picks," Dimar replied. "I do not think they could have torn down the boards with those."

"Then someone else must have done it," John concluded. "Didn't you say it was open when you first found it, and the next time you went it was boarded up?"

"Yes, Snowball went through the tunnel to the outdoors. That is how we happened to notice it," Sallie explained.

"And it was still closed when we saw the man and woman leave in a boat," Dimar added.

"Someone is messing around at that mine, John, and they could be dangerous," Elizabeth said nervously.

"I know," John agreed. "Well, Dimar, we should be on our way soon."

"Mr. Shaw, couldn't I go, too?" Celia asked.

"No, Celia," Uncle John replied. "Dimar knows how to get around in the woods. I'm afraid you'd get lost. Then we would have to go looking for you, too." He smiled.

"I would be glad to help find my friends," Sallie volunteered.

"Thanks, Sallie, but I believe Dimar will be enough help, along with Uncle Ned and Dr. Woodard," John replied, smiling at the girl. "I appreciate the concern of all you young people. If we do need you girls later, we'll let you know."

Hilda looked bewildered as she silently listened to the conversation.

Elizabeth rose from the table. "Perhaps we should pray first," she said. Bowing her head, she committed the search party to the Lord, asking Him to guide them and to bring Amanda and Joe safely home. When she finished, a chorus of amens echoed around the table.

"I'll get the lanterns," John stated.

"You know, John, I've been thinking about those ponies," Dr. Woodard said. "Don't you think we ought to take them back with us in case we find Joe and Amanda?"

"Well, yes, I guess you're right," John agreed.

"We find," Uncle Ned nodded. "Not come back till we find."

Bidding the others goodbye, the search party rode directly to the mine and tied up the ponies where they had found them. The men had hastily scanned the place on their previous search, but now they began looking more closely for clues.

"Let's go inside first and comb every inch of it," John suggested. "If there's nothing there, we'll search the tunnel and continue on through to the outside."

"I stay out here. Look for feet marks," Uncle Ned offered.

"All right, Uncle Ned. The rest of us will go inside," John decided.

After descending the steps into the mine, John, Dr. Woodard, and Dimar divided up the area and carefully searched by lantern light for any evidence that the missing young people had been there.

Suddenly Dimar straightened up. "I just remembered something," he said. "Mandie took that white cat with her. There may be paw prints."

"Amanda took Snowball with her? Her mother didn't mention that," Dr. Woodard said, stooping to inspect the dirt.

"You might know she would take Snowball. He goes with her almost everywhere except to church. And I have an idea she would like to take him to church if she thought she could get away with it." John Shaw laughed.

"But what good is it to look for footprints, really?"

asked Dr. Woodard. "All of you young people were here earlier, including Snowball."

"Here!" exclaimed Dimar, pointing ahead of him in the direction of the tunnel. "Footprints going into the tunnel. Big footprints."

John and Dr. Woodard hurried to look.

"You're right," John said. "I can see the print of Mandie's boots right there."

"And Joe's are right there." Dr. Woodard pointed. "But there are two sets of larger footprints right next to theirs as well. So they must be fresh footprints."

"Evidently a man and a woman," John observed.

"They must belong to the strange man and woman we saw leaving here," Dimar said. "They left in a boat outside the tunnel."

"Lead the way, Dimar. You're better at this than I am," John told the boy.

Dimar walked slowly through the tunnel, holding his lantern low in order to see the ground. As they came out into the daylight, they extinguished their lanterns and looked around. "The footprints continue this way," he said, bending low to look at the ground as he moved forward.

Something blue in a nearby bush caught his attention. He straightened up and started toward it. The men looked as he held up the blue sash.

"This is the sash to that dress they saw in the farmhouse. Mandie found this sash when we first went through the tunnel, and she has kept it in her apron pocket ever since," Dimar explained, handing it to John.

John and Dr. Woodard examined it. It did seem to be a sash to a lady's dress.

"That means Amanda dropped it here, probably on

purpose if she was carrying it in her apron pocket," John surmised.

"As an indication that she had been here," Dimar agreed.

Uncle Ned had worked his way around the mine and met up with the others. John showed him the sash and explained.

The old Indian quickly scanned the ground. "This way. To water," he told the others, slowly leading the way down to Rose Creek. Uncle Ned pointed out across the water. "Go in boat. No more feet marks," he said.

The search party stood at the edge of the creek, not sure what to do next. It would be almost impossible to trace a boat.

Chapter 8 / Adrift in the River

Mandie clutched both sides of the boat as it swirled this way and that, drifting out of Rose Creek into the mainstream of the Little Tennessee River. All the while, she tried to keep an eye on Joe, who was in the bottom of the boat, still not moving.

Snowball meowed and meowed as he was thrown around. Every time Mandie tried to catch him, the boat would swerve, and Snowball would fall beyond her reach.

Mandie kept praying. "Dear God," she said, "please don't let Joe die. Please help him. And dear God, please calm the water so we don't get upset and drowned. I'm so scared that we'll all fall out or the boat will wreck. Please help us! Please!"

As the wind continued to blow, the boat turned sharply and Snowball landed at Mandie's feet. She released one hand from the side of the boat and quickly snatched him up.

"Oh, Snowball, pretty kitty. I'm sorry you're so frightened," she whispered to the kitten as she buried her face in his soft white fur. "I'm scared, too, but we must trust God to save us, Snowball, because we sure can't save ourselves."

Above the sound of the water Mandie heard a groan behind her. She quickly managed to twist around enough to see Joe shake his head and try to sit up. "Joe! Joe! Are you all right now?" Mandie cried.

"You mean we aren't drowned yet?" he asked.

"Joe, what a thing to say," Mandie said, as inch by inch she managed to turn completely around facing him. "Are you really all right?"

Joe sat up and rubbed a hand across his face as he held on to the side of the boat with the other hand. "I suppose I'm all right, considering the situation we're in," the boy told her. "Are you all right?"

"Yes, now that I realize there is nothing I can do about it except trust God to save us," Mandie answered, holding tightly to Snowball with one hand.

"Is Snowball all right?" Joe asked, leaning forward to look at the frightened kitten.

"He's all right. He's just scared," Mandie replied.

"The last I remember, those people pushed us back into the boat and then shoved the boat out into the water and took the oars. What else happened?" he asked.

"You must have been knocked out. I was afraid you were going to die before we got rescued," she said solemnly. "What a terrible thing I have done. I caused all this trouble just by disobeying my mother."

Joe looked at her in silence for a moment. "I know we shouldn't have stopped at the mine, but I think we're getting enough punishment right now. I'm sure our parents will forgive us," he assured. "They'll be glad just to have us home in one piece—if we make it," he added.

Just then a big wave sloshed over the side of the boat, spraying them both as the boat rocked wildly.

"Oh, Joe!" Mandie cried, "nobody will ever find us

way out here in the middle of this river."

"I wish you could swim," said Joe. "We could probably jump out of this boat and swim to the bank."

"I am going to learn how to swim," Mandie firmly stated. "If I don't drown in this river, I am going to learn how to swim."

"It's about time. Most girls know how to swim by the time they're twelve years old," Joe teased.

Mandie ignored the jest. "I made the mistake of letting those mean people know I can't swim. Otherwise they might have at least left us on land somewhere," she said regretfully.

"I doubt that. They wanted us out of their way for a while, and this was the easiest way to do it," Joe said.

"What do you imagine they had in those bags?"

"I have no idea, but whatever it was, it must have been awfully valuable or important for them to go to all this trouble," Joe replied.

"They must have figured it was more valuable than our lives. They don't know but what we got drowned in this river with no oars to control the boat," Mandie said. "Who do you suppose they were?"

"They knew your uncle's name and that he owned the mine, so they must be from around Franklin somewhere," Joe answered. "I'd like to go after them and make them pay for this."

"No, Joe, we have to forgive them. You know that," Mandie reminded him.

"Well, anyway, I hope we never see them again," he muttered.

"Br-r-r-r!" Mandie shivered as she cuddled Snowball to her, still clutching to one side of the boat. "It's cold out here on this river. I'm getting chilled through and through."

"If we could sit together, we might be warmer. Maybe we could gradually move closer," he suggested. But when he started to get up, the boat rocked dangerously.

Mandie's heart pounded. "No!" she cried. "Don't stand up! The boat might turn over!"

Joe looked disappointed. "I'm sorry, Mandie. I wish I had a coat to give you."

"That's all right," Mandie replied. I don't think I'll freeze to death. By the way, where are we headed?"

"This river flows north from Georgia and then northwest right into Tennessee, where it goes into the Tennessee River," he told her. "So we might just end up in Tennessee if we keep on going."

"But that would take an awfully long time, wouldn't it? We aren't actually moving forward very fast. It's mostly the wiggly boat that makes it seem that way, don't you think?"

"I'd say it'd take quite a while to get there, but what else can we do but go on to Tennessee? We can't stop this boat and turn it around or even dock it at a riverbank."

"We can pray," Mandie suggested. "Prayer changes things, you know."

"We haven't said our verse," Joe reminded her.

"I did while you were knocked out, but we can say it again," Mandie offered.

Joe nodded.

Together they looked toward the sky and repeated, " 'What time I am afraid, I will put my trust in Thee.' "

"God will help us," Mandie assured her friend.

"I know. I just hope it's soon. I'm hungry," Joe moaned.

Suddenly the boat lurched and turned toward the river-bank, picking up speed. Then it slammed into the brush growing on the bank by the water.

"Grab something! Quick!" Joe cried. He stood up to snatch at the bushes. The boat almost turned over.

Mandie dropped Snowball in the bottom of the boat and tried to reach the limbs, ignoring the wobbling boat beneath her feet.

The boat kept swirling. Every time Mandie and Joe tried to grab the bushes, the boat would suddenly move too far away. Finally Joe managed to get a limb in his hand, but it was dead and broke right off the bush. Mandie snatched at the leaves on another branch, and the dead leaves crumbled away.

"Keep trying!" Joe yelled.

"I can't reach far enough to get hold of anything!" Mandie yelled back.

The boat moved a little nearer the bank. Then suddenly it whirled back out into the current. Mandie and Joe, thrown off balance by the quick movement, fell onto the seat together. The boat continued on down the river.

Joe bent to scoop up Snowball and handed him to Mandie.

"Oh, Joe, what a shame! We were so close to the bush but we couldn't reach it," Mandie said, her voice quivering.

"Maybe the boat will do that again," Joe encouraged. "And maybe next time we'll have better luck."

The boat continued on its way. So many trees grew along the riverbanks that it was impossible to see whether there were any houses or anyone who might happen to see them and come to their rescue. The leaves were turning yellow, orange, red and brown but were not yet falling from the trees. The two young people clung to the boat as the current swerved it about on the river.

"I didn't realize there were so many curves in this river," Mandie remarked as they rounded a big bend.

"That's probably because you've never been out on it before," Joe said.

"I hope this is the last time," Mandie replied as Snowball snuggled under her arm in fright.

When the river straightened out again, Joe suddenly pointed toward the trees. "Look!" he cried. "There's a man over there."

Mandie looked up. She tried waving but the rocking boat made it impossible for her to take her hand from the side. "Help! Help us!" she yelled as loudly as she could. But her cry was lost in the wind. The man didn't seem to notice, and the boat quickly moved on by.

"I don't think he heard you," Joe said.

"I know," Mandie replied. "We've got to do something! We can't just keep on going like this. We may be thrown out of the boat!"

"I know, but what can we do?" Joe asked, frustrated.

"We can pray again," Mandie suggested.

"You pray," Joe urged, looking toward the sky.

"Dear God, please help us!" Mandie began, looking toward the sky. "Please forgive me for all the trouble I've caused. I'm so sorry. Please help us get back to our parents. I know they're worried to death by now. Please forgive me, and please help us!"

"Amen," Joe added.

The wind blew strongly in their faces, and Mandie shivered a little.

"We'll be all right, Joe. I know God will help us," Mandie said.

As Mandie spoke, the boat slowed down and stopped wobbling, but it was still in the middle of the big river.

Mandie looked up into the sky. "Thank you, Lord! Thank you! Every little bit helps!"

Mandie looked at Joe. "I believe we're going to get out of this predicament somehow," she said.

"I think you're right, but I'm getting awfully hungry," Joe said.

At that moment the boat hit another strong current. It picked up speed and slammed around in the river.

Mandie gasped.

"Hold on!" Joe shouted.

The boat swirled and headed for the riverbank again.

"Grab something when we hit the bank!" Joe yelled.

"I'll try!" Mandie yelled back.

When the boat came close to the riverbank, the two waited for a chance to grab some of the bushes growing along the edge. The boat slowed down and hovered just out of reach of the limbs.

Mandie scanned the bushes. "I hear a dog, Joe. Listen."

The sound of barking rapidly grew louder.

"I hope someone is with the dog," Joe said, watching closely.

Just then a huge black-and-white shaggy dog jumped out of the bushes and sat on the edge of the riverbank, barking.

"Help! Help us!" Joe shouted.

The dog just sat there, barking. No one came to investigate.

Then the boat quickly turned and was pulled by the current out into the middle of the river again, causing Joe and Mandie to fall back down on the seat. Mandie grabbed the frightened kitten by the tail and pulled him onto her lap.

As the runaway boat raced down the river, Mandie and Joe looked at each other.

"God *will* save us," Mandie insisted in a nervous voice.

"It's just not time yet I guess," Joe surmised.

They smiled bravely, but the two grew colder and hungrier as they floated on down the river. Snowball never stopped meowing and hours seemed to go by.

Then all of a sudden, what they feared most happened! The boat slammed toward the riverbank again, striking an old dead limb sticking out into the water.

There was no time to think. The boat overturned, throwing Mandie and Joe into the water. Snowball leaped out, landing on the dead limb.

Mandie began to sink. "Help me!" Mandie coughed as she got a mouthful of water.

Joe, an expert swimmer, quickly swam to her side, grabbed hold of her, and tried to swim toward land.

"Get Snowball!" Mandie cried, pointing to the kitten perched on the dead limb.

When Joe tried to reach him, Snowball dashed up the log, hopped onto the land, and disappeared into the bushes.

"At least we know he didn't drown!" Joe yelled above the slosh of the water as he tried to tow Mandie to safety.

The overturned boat bounced around them and then suddenly struck them both hard. Both Joe and Mandie were stunned for a moment. Joe shook the water out of his eyes, held on to Mandie, and tried to make his way toward solid ground.

When they finally reached the safety of the bank, they

found the dirt so slippery that they had trouble climbing out of the water.

"I'll push you up," Joe offered. "Grab whatever you can up there so you won't fall back down."

Mandie nodded as Joe grabbed her firmly around the waist and shoved her upward. Mandie grasped at the weeds on the bank, but they came uprooted in her hands, and she fell back down into the water.

"Sorry, Joe," she gasped.

"Try again," Joe urged, giving her another boost.

Mandie reached again but could not catch hold of a thing. She started crying and slid back down, floundering in the water.

"I'm going to drown!" she screamed, becoming hysterical.

"No!" Joe slapped her cheek with a wet hand.

Mandie instantly stopped crying and stared at him.

"I'm sorry, but I had to do that. Now grab something this time—anything. Just grab something," Joe commanded.

Mandie took a deep breath and nodded.

Joe pushed her up out of the water again. This time Mandie grasped the strong limb of a bush and managed to scramble up the slippery bank, slipping and falling in the wet mud. Joe pulled himself up out of the water and the two worked their way up to firm ground where they fell, exhausted and chilled to the bone.

"Thank you, dear God," Mandie whispered as she passed out right there in the weeds.

Gasping for breath, Joe, too, lost consciousness.

The wind blew hard, and the air became colder, but

the two young people didn't feel a thing. As the sky dimmed, the overturned boat floated downstream and finally sank.

Mandie and Joe did not stir.

Chapter 9 / Forgiveness

The men were still at the mine, debating what to do next after Uncle Ned had assured them the footprints led directly to a boat.

"Why don't we split up?" John Shaw suggested. "Dr. Woodard, can you whistle really loud?"

Dr. Woodard placed two fingers in his mouth and answered with a loud, piercing whistle.

"Fine," said Uncle John. "Would you stay here at the mine in case Joe and Amanda come back. You can give us a whistle, and we'll be back in a flash."

Dr. Woodard agreed.

"Uncle Ned, maybe you can search upstream and Dimar can come with me," John continued. "We'll go in opposite directions along the banks of the river to see if we can spot a boat."

"Take lanterns," Uncle Ned suggested, picking up one of the lanterns by the mine.

"Good idea," John replied. "It's not dark yet, but it might be before we get back, so we'll divide up the lanterns among us."

Dimar picked up one and left the third for Dr. Woodard. "I will carry this one for us," Dimar offered.

"I'll be glad to stay here and wait for Joe and Amanda," Dr. Woodard said. "Since they left their ponies, maybe they will come back here—if they can." There was a slight tremor in his voice as he spoke.

"We find them," Uncle Ned assured the doctor.

"I'd say that we should turn back when the sun starts to go down," John suggested. "By that time we will have walked a good distance, and if we don't find them by then, we'll get a boat and go out on the river."

"You don't have a boat around here anywhere, do you?" Dr. Woodard asked.

"No, we'll have to ride a long way down the river to the dock where I keep one. It's too far to walk right now," John replied.

Uncle Ned handed Dr. Woodard his rifle. "Take gun," he said.

Dr. Woodard started to refuse.

"Uncle Ned is right," John assured him. "We don't know what kind of people we're dealing with. You may have to use it."

"But I don't think I could—"

"Have the rifle ready anyway, just in case," John stated. "It is loaded, isn't it?"

Uncle Ned nodded. "Ready," he said.

"I hope that's not necessary," John replied. "If you see or hear anything at all, Doctor, give us your whistle."

Dr. Woodard agreed.

" 'Nuff talk. Go! Make haste!" Uncle Ned headed upstream.

"Come on, Dimar," said Uncle John. "We're on our way."

Dimar nodded and took the lead through the bushes.

As he and John walked downstream, they checked the bank all along the way for signs of a boat. It was slow going. The brush was thick, and there was a constant scurrying and chirping as rabbits, squirrels, and chipmunks evaded them. The birds flew high up into the trees to fuss at the men invading their domain.

John looked around overhead and laughed. "With all that noise, we certainly couldn't slip up on anyone, could we?"

"I will tell them to be quiet," Dimar said. He stopped and gave several different kinds of whistles.

To John's amazement the birds hushed. He could no longer hear the animals moving about. "You are a gifted person, Dimar. They wouldn't have done that for me."

Dimar shrugged his shoulders. "I only told them that we must be quiet."

John looked sharply at the boy. "You *told* them that?"

"I spoke in their language. I have learned the different sounds they use," Dimar explained, walking on.

"That is a remarkable achievement," John said. "Don't ever lose it."

Dimar smiled.

After they had walked quite a distance, the Indian boy stopped to listen. John stopped also, watching Dimar. He, too, heard something. It sounded like a dog barking in the distance.

"It is coming from up ahead," said Dimar.

As they walked on, the sound grew louder. It was definitely a dog barking. It sounded like a big dog.

Dimar stopped again and peered through the bushes with John looking over his shoulder. A big black-and-white shaggy dog was sitting there, barking at the trunk of a large chestnut tree. The two looked around. There was no one in sight.

Seeing the people, the dog ran downstream through the bushes, still barking loudly, causing a great commotion among the animals and birds in the forest.

"He must have treed a squirrel," John said.

"Crazy dog to run away from us and to keep on barking," Dimar decided.

Little did they know that downstream, Amanda and Joe were lying unconscious on the bank, oblivious to the frantic search for them.

As Uncle Ned searched the creek bank upstream, he carefully combed the bushes for any clue to the missing young people. Nothing would escape Uncle Ned's keen observation. But there was no sign of anyone or any other clue.

"I promise Jim Shaw I watch over Papoose," he fumed to himself. "Papoose lost. Must find."

He checked his arrows in the sling to be sure he was prepared for any trouble that might arise, then stopped to look at the sun to judge the time of day.

Uncle Ned had not agreed with John that they should walk the banks, but he had not expressed his disagreement. The young people were not on the riverbanks. They had left by boat. The more he thought about it, the more he was sure they should call for help from the Cherokees. If he, and John, and Dimar didn't find them soon, he would talk to John about getting the Cherokees' help.

Mandie and Joe still lay on the river bank miles downstream. Though the wind had partially dried their clothes and hair, it had also chilled their bodies more. But they were so exhausted, they weren't aware of anything—least of all that someone else was pursuing them.

The man and woman who had set them adrift rode on horseback, the horses having found their way home.

As the couple carefully scanned the river for the two young people, the woman said, "I'm glad you changed your mind. It ain't right to do such a thing to younguns what ain't done nothin' to us. I jest hope they's all right."

"Yeah, I s'pose we did act a little hasty," the man agreed, riding alongside her.

"We's both brung up better than that and you know it," the woman said. "The Lord Almighty is goin' to have a hard time forgivin' us, I can guarantee you that."

"We told Him we's sorry. I ain't done that in coon's ages," the man said.

"Yeah, and now we gotta find them younguns and make sure they's all right."

"I s'pose you're right, Woman. I can look back now and see whut we been doin' ain't done us no good, so we might as well try it t'other way—fer a while anyway."

"Not jest for a while, but from here on," the woman argued. "If you don't straighten up with me and try to do right, I ain't havin' nothin' else to do with you. The Lord don't require a woman to live with a man that jest won't live right."

"Woman, don't you talk that way. You been my wife for purty nigh forty years," the man said.

"And that's goin' to be purty nigh forty years long 'nuff if you don't change your way of livin'," the woman replied.

The man frowned at her. "You don't care nothin' 'bout me no more?"

"It ain't that atall," she responded. "But we's gittin' old, and one day we's gotta go meet our Maker. If we don't start doin' better, we ain't gonna see Him. We'll be goin' t'other way. I hope you been thinkin' 'bout that."

"Yep, s'pose I have," the old man said. "And I do still love ya, so I s'pose I'll hafta change my ways. To tell you the truth, I'm glad you got on this path of righteousness. I couldn't uh done it by myself."

"If we hadn't met up with that sweet little girl, I don't think I'd uh been thinkin' 'bout our way of livin'. She jest made me realize what a terrible hole we's got ourselves into," the woman said. "I sure hope we find them young-guns and they's all right. I won't never be able to forgive myself if they's not."

They traveled on, searching along the riverbank. The wrecked boat was already beneath the water down-stream, but as they rounded a bend, they spotted the young people lying on the ground in the weeds ahead.

The woman gasped and jumped down from her horse before the animal had completely stopped. She rushed to the young people, and the man followed.

"Thank the Lord, they're alive!" exclaimed the woman, bending over Mandie. "They don't seem to be hurt none. I think they's jest asleep."

Hearing someone talking above her, Mandie forced her eyes open. Seeing the man and woman standing over her, she was afraid to speak. Unable to tell whether the old people had come to do more harm or what, she only stared at them and tried to straighten her cold, stiff arms. She shivered from the penetrating cold. Just then Joe opened his eyes and sat up quickly as he saw the old couple. "*Now* what do you want?" he demanded, moving protectively to Mandie's side.

"We want somethin' from you," the old man said, looking down at his feet.

"Something from us?" Mandie questioned.

"We want your forgiveness," the woman said sadly. "We's sorry, truly sorry, for what we's done, and we want to ask your forgiveness."

Mandie and Joe looked at each other, unbelieving.

"Why?" Joe demanded.

"Because like this here young lady told us, we gotta forgive and ask for forgiveness if we wanna git through them pearly gates up there," the woman replied. "My pa was a preacher. He learnt his children what he knowed 'bout the Bible. He'd be ashamed of me right now. It jest seemed so easy to stray from the straight and narrow path."

Mandie reached for the woman's hand and squeezed it. "I know what you mean. That's how we got into all this trouble. I strayed down the wrong path and broke a promise to my mother. I'm awfully ashamed of myself," Mandie told her.

"Well, are you younguns willin' to forgive us?" the man asked.

"Of course," Joe said. "We have to."

"Have to?" the man questioned.

"Joe means that the Bible says if we don't forgive others, our heavenly Father won't forgive us. And we sure have a lot of trespasses ourselves to be forgiven for," Mandie explained. "I told you when you left us that we forgave you, and we really do."

"Yes, we do," Joe added.

The woman took Mandie in her arms, and the man firmly grasped Joe's shoulder.

"We thank you for givin' us a chance to live better," the man said. "We was afraid you'd really make it hard for us. You had a right to."

"What can we do 'bout gittin' you younguns home now?" the old woman asked.

"We left our ponies back at the mine," Mandie told them.

"They may still be there, but I imagine everyone is out looking for us by now," said Joe as he noticed the sun sinking in the sky.

"Yes, I'm surprised Uncle Ned hasn't found us yet," Mandie said, trying to stand. "Oh, I'm so cold I can't stand up."

Joe managed to get to his feet and helped her stand.

Suddenly Mandie gasped. "Where is Snowball?" she cried, looking around. "Snowball, where are you? Kitty! Kitty! Where are you?"

Joe helped her search the bushes, and the old couple joined in the search, too. But the white kitten was nowhere to be found.

"Mandie, I think we'd better go home and get some help to find him," Joe said. "That way our parents will know we're safe."

"I guess you're right, Joe, but I hate to leave here without finding him," Mandie said with tears in her eyes.

"We'll come back," Joe promised. "Besides, maybe Snowball went home. You know he's a smart cat. He could find the way home."

Mandie smiled at Joe. "If he's able, he'll find the way home," she said.

"Come on," the woman said to Mandie, "you're cold. We's got blankets on the horses. You ride with me. The boy can ride with him."

"Oh, will I be glad to get home again!" Mandie exclaimed as the woman helped her up on the horse with her.

The woman wrapped a warm blanket around Mandie, and the man did likewise for Joe. Then they were on their way.

As they rode along, Mandie's curiosity grew. "Why did you do what you did to us?" she asked.

"It's really a bad mixed-up mess," the woman began. "We cain't make no livin' no more. Jest ain't no way to do it. We worked the land long as we could. Nuthin' wouldn't grow. We jest plain didn't have nuthin' to eat and nowheres to git it," the woman said.

"I wish I had known," Mandie said. "I'd have seen to it that you had something to eat."

"Well, I don't know whut a youngun like you could do, but anyway, we figured the only way we could keep from starvin' to death was jest to take 'nuff to live on. And that's all we's been takin', jest 'nuff to live on," she repeated.

"From where?" Mandie asked, huddling within the warm blanket.

"To begin with, we'd jest take a pig here and a few things there, from various places, like I said—jest barely 'nuff to stay alive. And then we found out 'bout that gold mine over in Buncombe County. So we went over there and took out a little gold when nobody was watchin'," the woman explained.

"You've been stealing gold?" Mandie questioned.

"Guess you'd call it that, even though we was only takin' 'nuff to buy somethin' to eat," the old woman said. "Anyhow we still got it in the bags. We ain't made 'way with it." She patted the bags hanging across the horse.

"Then you must return it," Mandie told her. "The Bible says, 'Thou shalt not steal.' That's one of the Ten Commandments."

"I know all 'bout that, but when you git so hungry your

stomach seems like it's stuck to your backbone, you're liable to do anythin' to git somethin' to eat," she tried to explain.

Mandie patted the woman's hand. "I'm sorry you've been hungry when we have so much to eat," she said. "Y'all just come home with us. I know my Uncle John will see to it that y'all have something to eat from now on."

Joe was asking similar questions of the old man, but the man was more proud, more reluctant to divulge his personal affairs. Yet at Joe's insistence, he finally told all.

"Couldn't you find any work to do?" Joe asked.

"Naw, too old. Nobody don't want old men like me when they kin git young able-bodied workers," the man said.

"That's not fair. You have to eat the same as the young men," Joe protested. "If you and your wife will go back to Mandie's uncle's house with us, I think my father and her uncle can find something honest for y'all to do."

"I know John Shaw," the old man told him. "But I ain't never had to ask a favor from nobody in my life."

"It's better to ask a favor and be honest than to go doing things like y'all have been doing," Joe told him.

"We'll see," the man replied.

The sky was dimming as they rode up to the mine. The surrounding trees made it darker there than in the wide open spaces.

But when they reached the mine, they were greeted by Dr. Woodard, pointing a rifle at them and giving a loud whistle.

"Don't shoot! It's us!" Joe cried, quickly slipping down from the man's horse. He ran to his father's side.

Dr. Woodard, surprised, hugged his son with one arm. "Where have you and Amanda been?" he asked as Mandie jumped down from the woman's horse and joined him.

"Everything is all right now," Joe told him.

"Yes, Dr. Woodard, we've come to get our ponies," Mandie explained. "These people need help. They're going home with us."

"Amanda, don't you know who these people are?" Dr. Woodard asked. "This is Jake Burns and his wife."

"Jake Burns? The man who is going to buy the mine from Uncle John?" Mandie asked.

Dr. Woodard nodded, never taking his eyes off the couple.

Mandie turned to the man. "But you said you don't even have enough to eat. How can you have the money to buy this mine?"

"I know it don't make no sense," Jake replied. "We figured we'd have 'nuff gold to buy this mine and that old farmhouse over there in the trees. This is good farming land. We could make a living here without even minin'."

"But you stole that gold and you must return it," Mandie insisted.

"I know. You're right," Jake said, hanging his head.

Dr. Woodard cleared his throat. "Jake Burns, I'm going to see to it that you get what's coming to—"

"No, Dr. Woodard," Mandie interrupted. "We know they've been bad, but we promised them forgiveness," she said quickly.

"We will see," Dr. Woodard replied, finally lowering the rifle. "Your Uncle John is going to have something to say about this."

"Then let's go home," Mandie said.

"We'll wait for John and the others first," said Dr. Woodard.

In a moment John and Dimar came hurrying through the bushes from one direction and Uncle Ned from the other.

"We were on the way back when we heard your whistle," John said, seeing Joe and Mandie and the old couple. "Mandie, Joe, are you all right?"

"Yes, sir," Mandie said, running into his waiting arms.

"Thank Big God Papoose not hurt," Uncle Ned declared.

John Shaw looked confused. "Jake, Ludie, how did you get here?"

"That's a long story, Uncle John. We'll explain when we get home," Mandie told him.

"Well, let's get going," he said.

Uncle Ned was the last to mount. "Jake Burns bad man. Must punish," he mumbled.

Chapter 10 / Explanations

Jason Bond had been constantly on the lookout for the search party to return, so when he saw them coming, he hurried to assist with the horses and ponies as they stopped at the gate.

The caretaker smiled at Mandie and reached to help her dismount. "I reckon I'm awfully glad to see you home, Missy. And you, too, young fella," he said, grinning at Joe.

"You just don't know how glad we are to be back," Mandie said, painfully dismounting her pony. Her arms and legs were bruised from being knocked around in the boat, and she ached all over.

"At one point we kinda doubted that we'd ever get back," Joe said, handing his pony's reins to Mr. Bond.

Elizabeth, hearing the horses' hoofs and the voices, came running to the front door. Everyone in the house crowded behind her to wait for the group coming up the walkway.

Mandie ran straight to her mother's arms, and Joe, who was always reserved, went straight to his mother and put his arm around her.

"Amanda, we've been praying for y'all to get home

117

safely. Are you all right?" Elizabeth asked with tears in her eyes. She hugged her daughter tightly. "Where on earth have you been, darling?"

"I'm sorry, Mother. I have a lot of forgiveness to ask," Mandie admitted. She looked up at Celia and Sallie. "Has Snowball come home?" she asked.

"No, I don't think so," Celia replied. "Has anyone seen him?"

As a chorus of nos came from the group, Mandie's blue eyes filled with tears. "Oh, Mother, I've lost Snowball. I couldn't find him in the woods."

Realizing the condition her daughter was in, Elizabeth delayed any more talk. "There, there, Amanda," she said, patting her daughter on the back. "Straight to the bathtub and then some hot food. After that we'll sit down and talk this whole thing out."

"I go help," Liza spoke up from behind Elizabeth.

With a heavy heart, Mandie trudged up the stairs as Liza followed.

"You, too, Joe," Mrs. Woodard told her son, tousling his windblown hair.

Dimar volunteered to go with Joe, and Joe seemed grateful. "This is going to be a big job to get back in shape again," he said.

Mandie was so worn out and hungry that she almost fell into her room when Liza opened the door for her.

The Negro girl caught her by the arm and led her over to the bed to sit down. "First we git dis here fire goin'," Liza said, lighting the wood in the fireplace. Then she turned back to Mandie. "Now off wid dese filthy, wet clothes, Missy," she ordered.

As Liza helped the girl get undressed, Mandie gave a big sigh. "I could just curl up in bed. I'm so tired," she told Liza.

"Now you finish takin' off dem clothes whilst I fix de water fo' you," said Liza. "And don't you go to sleep. Git dem other things off." She hurried into the bathroom to prepare the bath.

As Mandie limply finished undressing, Liza rushed back, snatched a robe from a hanger, put it around Mandie, and hurried her into the bathroom.

The warm water revived Mandie, and she agreed to let Liza wash her dirty, tangled hair.

Liza helped her into clean clothes and sat her down by the fireplace. Then while Liza gently brushed Mandie's long blonde hair, Mandie began to talk. She told the girl everything that had happened since she and Joe had left that morning.

Liza related the day's events at the house. "Yo' ma, and dat doctuh's wife, dey been wringin' der hands all dis day long," she told Mandie. "And everybody else been sittin' 'round like somebody died. After de men went to de Hadleys and come back wid dat Hilda girl and no sign of y'all, things been awful here."

"Liza, isn't my hair dry enough to go downstairs?" Mandie asked impatiently. "I'm starving to death. We haven't had a bite to eat since breakfast."

"I 'spect so, Missy, if we don't braid it up. Let's jest tie it back wid a ribbon so's it kin finish dryin'," she suggested, reaching for a ribbon and tying the heavy, long blonde hair back.

Mandie went downstairs and as she entered the parlor, Joe called to her from the settee. "Come over here," Mandie. He patted the seat next to him. The young people were all hovering around Joe, asking him questions.

"Ah, Mandie," Celia said, "Joe has told us what happened. You must be exhausted."

Mandie looked around the room. Hilda was huddled in a corner, watching and listening, Sallie sat in a plush chair nearby, and Jake and his wife seemed to be in serious conversation with Uncle John and the other adults.

As Mandie sat down, Elizabeth came over to them. "Aunt Lou has food on the table for you two," she said. "Everyone else has already eaten. Go on in to the dining room. I'll be in before you get finished."

"Yes, ma'am," Mandie and Joe replied together. They rose and did as they were told.

Aunt Lou hovered over them, making sure that they ate a hearty meal. "My chile, you got to eat up. You gonna be sick if you don't after all dat trouble out on dat river, gittin' wet and cold and all dat," the big old Negro woman told Mandie. "And you, too, young man. I don't want no sick people on my hands."

Mandie swallowed a mouthful of mashed potatoes and laughed at her concern. "Aunt Lou, Joe's father is a doctor, remember? If we get sick, he will doctor us. You won't have to worry about it."

"Now, my chile, you know I hafta look after you. I took you for my chile dat fust day when you come here, all poor and hungry from dat cabin out in de country." Aunt Lou walked around behind the girl and reached to put more potatoes on her plate.

Mandie protested. "Aunt Lou, I can't eat any more potatoes. Please don't stuff me. I'll have nightmares."

The Negro woman turned to Joe and put the spoonful of potatoes on his plate. "You gotta eat, too," she told him. "Git some mo' of dat beefstew. Jenny made it jest right." She pulled the big bowl closer to Joe and stood there while he spooned a big helping onto his plate.

Joe looked up at her mischievously. "Is that enough?"

"Maybe fo' now," Aunt Lou said. "Both of you drink up dat milk. It'll make you sleep good."

Mandie sighed and picked up her glass. "I'd really rather go to bed than eat," she said.

"Too early to go to bed," the old woman said. "Git yo' sleepin' hours all mixed up and git up too early. 'Sides, you got guests to see to."

"I think we've already entertained them enough today," Joe spoke up. "With all that's happened, it's time to rest."

Mandie laid down her fork. "Aunt Lou, I just can't eat any more," she said with a quiver in her voice. "I've been thinking about Snowball. He's lost somewhere, and he's probably hungry."

Aunt Lou immediately put her big arm around the girl, and Mandie buried her face in the woman's apron, bursting into tears.

Joe jumped up and came around the table to take Mandie's hand in his. "Don't cry, Mandie. I know how much Snowball means to you. We'll find him somehow," he assured her.

"There's no way to find him," she sobbed as Aunt Lou stroked Mandie's thick blonde hair.

When Elizabeth entered the room, she rushed to Mandie's side. Mandie released Aunt Lou, and Joe handed her his handkerchief.

"What's wrong, dear?" Elizabeth asked, putting an arm around her daughter's shaking shoulders.

Mandie took a deep breath, trying to control her voice. "I've lost Snowball for good, and it's all my fault!" she cried.

Joe stepped back, and Elizabeth pulled out a chair to sit next to Mandie. Joe quietly slipped out the door, and Aunt Lou followed.

"We'll search for him tomorrow, dear," Elizabeth said.

"Mother, I know you're angry with me for disobeying you," Mandie cried. "If I hadn't disobeyed, none of these terrible things would have happened. I'm so sorry. I've asked God to forgive me, too."

"I'm not angry with you, Amanda," Elizabeth said. "I'm hurt because you didn't keep your promise to go straight to the Hadleys and back without stopping anywhere. But hurt and anger are two different things." Elizabeth gave her daughter a hug. "Oh, Amanda, I just love you so much, it hurts me to see you getting into trouble."

Mandie looked into her mother's blue eyes, so much like her own. "I'm sorry, Mother. I don't want to ever hurt you. It's just that we saw some horses tied up by the mine, and I asked Joe if we could stop and see who was there. He didn't want to, but he finally agreed. I didn't know it was going to turn into such a terrible thing. Please forgive me, Mother."

"I do forgive you, Amanda," Elizabeth said. "But please, please try a little harder to act more mature. You must learn to think twice when you're tempted to break promises and disobey."

"I'll really try hard," Mandie said, reaching up to embrace her mother.

"To help you remember," Elizabeth continued, "I have decided to confine you to the house for the rest of the holidays unless an adult is with you. You will not be going anywhere with your friends unless there is a grownup who can go with you. Is that understood?"

"Yes, Mother. I understand," Mandie replied.

"That is rather mild punishment for what you've done, but I can guarantee you that if you disobey me again, the punishment will be much worse," Elizabeth warned.

"Those people have told us all about what happened. I'm thankful that you and Joe weren't harmed more than you were."

Mandie looked up into her mother's face with concern. "You and Uncle John will help those people, won't you?"

Elizabeth answered slowly. "That's the Christian thing to do, of course, but they will have to prove that they are sincere about changing their way of living."

Mandie smiled. "Thanks, Mother. I told them you would help."

"Now, if you're finished eating, I think we should go back to the parlor. Your friends are waiting for you," Elizabeth said, rising from her chair.

Mandie followed her mother back to the parlor. As she entered the room Uncle John called to Mandie, "Come over here for a minute, Amanda."

Mandie walked past the group of young people to the other end of the room where the adults and Joe sat talking. "Yes, sir?" she responded.

"Sit down, Amanda. We need to talk a little while," Uncle John told her, indicating a nearby chair. "Jake and his wife, Ludie, have been telling us what went on today," Uncle John began as Mandie sat down.

Mandie turned to the couple sitting next to Uncle John. "Did you tell them everything?"

"Everything that was necessary," Jake answered.

"But everything was necessary," Mandie insisted.

"We didn't think it was necessary to tell him about our personal affairs," Jake said.

"But you must tell him everything, Mr. Burns," Mandie replied. "If you don't, then I will. Uncle John needs to know."

"Amanda!" Uncle John rebuked her for her sharp words. "They told us about finding you and Joe at the mine and leaving you in that boat, and then coming back to rescue you. They said you and Joe had forgiven them, so what else could I do but forgive them. It just better not happen again."

Dr. Woodard agreed. "I guess I feel the same way," he said reluctantly.

"Did you tell Uncle John about the gold?" Mandie asked Ludie.

Ludie looked down at her wrinkled hands. "No, we can take care of returnin' that ourselves," she replied.

"I know you can return it yourselves, but what are you going to do for a living?" Mandie asked.

"You don't have the money to buy the mine," Joe reminded them.

The couple sat humbled in front of John Shaw and Dr. Woodard. Uncle Ned silently watched them with a sullen expression on his face.

"We'll jest have to trust in the Lord," Ludie said. "He won't let us starve."

Uncle John spoke up. "Are you not planning to buy the mine now, Jake?" he asked.

Jake shuffled his threadworn boots on the carpet. "Ain't got no money now," he replied, avoiding John's gaze.

"Ain't no use beatin' 'round the bush 'bout it, Jake," Ludie said. "We've gotta be honest 'bout everythin'." She turned to John. "We's taken 'nuff gold from another mine to pay for your mine, Mr. Shaw. But now we's realized the sin we's committed, so we's gotta return the gold to its rightful owner."

John looked from Jake to Ludie in surprise. "You

mean you just took gold out of someone's mine?"

"That's jest what we did," Ludie replied. "And after these here younguns showed us the error of our ways, we's decided we'd better straighten up and try to live right. So we's gonna return the gold."

"My goodness, Jake!" Uncle John exclaimed. "I had no idea you didn't have the money to buy the mine when you asked about it."

"And that's not all, Mr. Shaw," Joe added. "They don't even have any money to live on or any way to make a living."

"They've been going hungry," Mandie added. "Joe and I thought maybe you and Dr. Woodard could figure out some way to help them."

Dr. Woodard looked concerned. "John, there must be some way we can help."

"Jake, why didn't you come to me and let me know you were so hard up?" John asked. "Your father was a loyal worker for my father in that ruby mine, and you helped, too, I believe. You must know I'd do anything I can for you and your wife. You don't have to go taking other people's gold as long as I'm around."

Mandie and Joe looked at each other and smiled. Everything was working out just the way they wanted it to.

"I ain't never had to ask a favor of no man," Jake grumbled.

"That wouldn't be asking a favor. It would be giving me a chance to return my appreciation for your father's work," John said. He looked at Dr. Woodard. "Now what can we arrange?"

Dr. Woodard thought for a moment. "Where do y'all live now?" he asked.

"We ain't got no home right now. We was rentin' the old Tittle farm, but we couldn't make a livin' off it, much less pay the rent," Ludie said.

John and Dr. Woodard exchanged glances.

Mandie's eyes sparkled. "What about the old farmhouse you own, Uncle John, over near the mine—the one where we found the dress? No one lives there."

"That's a good idea, Amanda, except we've got to find some work for these people so they can make a living," Uncle John agreed.

"They told us the land around the mine was good farming land. That was why they wanted to buy the mine, just to get the land to farm," Joe spoke up.

Uncle John turned to Jake. "Do you really think that land is any good to grow anything?"

"It sure is, John. It's fertile land. It oughta grow some good corn, and beans, and a few other things," Jake replied.

"What about the mine, Uncle John?" Mandie asked. "Couldn't they work the mine for you, too, after we get through with it?"

"Is the mine worth working, Jake?" Uncle John asked. "You ought to know. You were there when it was closed."

Uncle Ned gave a loud grunt, and Jake stirred uneasily in his chair.

"I really don't know, John. We's been going through your mine lately, but we didn't disturb nothin', so I don't know," Jake answered.

"Well, why don't we try it and see?" Uncle John asked. "I've already had it opened and had all the necessary repairs made."

"We should make a list of things we need to do," Dr. Woodard said, pulling a note pad and fountain pen from his vest pocket. "The house needs repairing." He began to write.

"Jake can paint and repair it in place of paying rent to begin with. I'll give him the paint and whatever he needs," Uncle John said.

"Does it have any furniture in it?" Dr. Woodard wanted to know. "They said they don't have anything."

"No, there's not a stick of anything in it," Mandie spoke up. "Uncle John, you've got a whole lot of furniture in the attic that you don't use. Could we take some of it to their house?"

"I'll help," Joe volunteered.

Uncle John smiled at the young people's concern. "That's exactly what we'll do. And Jake, I'll see that you get some pigs, and chickens, and feed, and seed. Now don't protest. We'll work things out so y'all can do enough work to cover everything. Don't think this is charity."

The old couple looked at each other, speechless, with tears in their eyes.

Ludie reached for Mandie's hand. "The Lord will take care of us, won't He?" she said to Mandie. "Soon as we trusted in Him, He started taking care of us."

"That's right, Mrs. Burns." Mandie smiled. "I'm so glad you and Mr. Burns decided to change your way of living. We'll do all we can to help you. I'll even ask Aunt Lou to make you a new dress."

"Oh, my! This dress I have on!" the old woman exclaimed, looking down at the blue gingham she was wearing. "It ain't rightly mine."

"Where did you get it?" Mandie asked.

"We took one little piece of the gold to buy it. I ain't never had a store-bought dress in my life. And I ain't had a new dress in twenty years. But then, I guess I don't have one now, neither, 'cause this dress ain't rightly mine, is it?" the woman rambled on.

"Whose mine did you get that gold out of?" Uncle John asked.

"The Tittles' mine. You see they moved out of their old place when they discovered that gold, and they built a big new house. We was rentin' the old one," Jake replied.

"When we take the gold back, I do hope they don't put us in jail," said Ludie.

"They could," Uncle John told her. "But I'll go with y'all to take it back, and we'll see what we can work out. I know Ed Tittle."

"But what about the dress?" Ludie asked.

"I don't imagine they'd want to take your dress, Mrs. Burns," Mandie assured her.

"But it was bought with their gold," Ludie said.

"I'll pay Ed Tittle for it, and you can work to pay that off, too," John said. "Now you can stay in this house long enough for us to get that farmhouse in livable condition."

Ludie's eyes grew wide in disbelief. "Live here?" she asked, looking around at all the Shaws' finery.

"We'll get some livestock," Uncle John continued, "and then we'll get the mine working. And come to think of it, Ludie, I believe we could use some extra help about the house with all the company we have right now."

"Thank you, Mr. Shaw. From the bottom of my heart, I thank you," Ludie said. "Jest tell me what you want done. I'll be more than glad to do anything you say."

Uncle Ned shook his head and grunted to himself. "Sad, bad mine. Jake Burns know it."

Mandie thought she heard the old Indian speak, and she turned to look at him. "Uncle Ned, you must have known Mr. Burns back when the mine was open," she said.

"Ummm," Uncle Ned grunted, giving Jake a mean look. "Father of Jake Burns close mine for father of John Shaw. No good to open."

Uncle John frowned at the old Indian. "Uncle Ned, I do wish you'd tell me what you've got against opening that mine."

Uncle Ned shook his head again. "Jake Burns there. He know why mine closed."

Jake shuffled his feet and wouldn't look at the Indian.

"Do you know why it was closed, Jake?" Uncle John asked. "Was it mined dry? Is that the secret?"

"Well, no. I didn't know everythin' that was goin' on," Jake replied. "I was only a boy at that time."

"All right, then. We'll work it and see if it yields anything," John said. Turning to Mandie, he asked, "Would you please ask Aunt Lou to get a room ready for these people and to let me know when she's finished. Then you and Joe can go back to your friends over there. I know they're all waiting to hear more about the day's events."

Mandie and Joe jumped up.

"Yes, sir, Uncle John," Mandie said as she and Joe rushed out of the room.

They found Aunt Lou in the dining room overseeing Liza as the girl cleaned off the table.

"Aunt Lou, Uncle John says to ask you to get a room opened up for Mr. and Mrs. Burns. They're going to be staying here until we get the old farmhouse by the mine fixed up for them to live in," she explained.

Aunt Lou thought for a moment. "Well now, it'll have to be de third flo'," she said. "Wid all dis comp'ny and everything, de second flo' is plum filled up, and de third flo' ain't too fancy."

"That's all right, Aunt Lou. They're going to work for Uncle John. He said Ludie could help here in the house, so I suppose he'll talk to you about that later," Mandie replied. Then catching hold of the big black woman's hand, she asked, "Aunt Lou, could you please make a new dress for Mrs. Burns? She hasn't had a new dress in twenty years."

"Ain't had a new dress in twenty years? My chile, whut in dis world she been wearin'?"

Mandie and Joe glanced at each other, and Joe replied, "She's wearing a borrowed dress right now. They're poor people."

"I guess I could make a plain one, but she'll hafta help," Aunt Lou said. Then she saw Liza leaning against the wall, listening. "Liza, git a move on!" she scolded. "We's gotta go find a room for dem Burns people and air it out."

"Thank you, Aunt Lou," Mandie said, squeezing the woman's dark hand.

"Git out o' here, my chile. Git back to yo' comp'ny," Aunt Lou said. "I'se got work to do."

As Mandie and Joe returned to the parlor, they were immediately surrounded by the other young people. Hilda was still sitting quietly, listening and watching.

Once again Joe and Mandie had to relate the day's events to their friends, covering every detail, even though by now everyone knew what had happened.

"I wish I could have been with you in that boat, Mandie," Celia said.

"Well, I wouldn't have," Sallie said.

"They could have been drowned," Dimar added.

"What are you going to do about Snowball?" Celia asked.

Mandie's face crumpled as she replied in a low, shaky voice, "I don't know. I guess I've lost him."

"We will find him," Sallie told her.

"But I haven't seen him since we got out of the water when the boat wrecked. He ran off into the bushes. We looked and looked, and we couldn't find any sign of him. I thought maybe he would come home, but . . ."

"He's got to be somewhere," Celia said.

"We will go and look for him tomorrow, Mandie," Dimar promised.

That night as Mandie said her prayers with Celia and Sallie, she pleaded with God. "Please send Snowball home to me, and let him be all right. Please, dear God, take care of him and send him home. Please!"

"Please!" Sallie echoed.

"Yes, please!" Celia added.

And in the darkness of the bedroom Hilda repeated, "Yes, please!"

Chapter 11 / A Mysterious Find

Everyone pitched in the next day to help Jake and Ludie Burns get settled. The boys helped the men hammer and repair the old farmhouse and then paint the inside. The girls donned aprons, tied sca. es over their hair, and had a glorious time going through all the dusty old furniture in the attic, choosing which pieces they would take to the Burnses' house.

"We can pick whatever we want to give them," Mandie said. "But Mother says Uncle John will have to approve anything we give away. Some of the furniture up here is old and valuable."

"This is a great idea," Celia exclaimed as she rummaged through the drawers of an old chest. "It's like having our own house and filling it with the furniture of our choice."

Sallie bent over an opened trunk containing books. "How much are we allowed to give them?" she asked.

"I suppose they'll need enough to fill up the house," Mandie said as she pulled old dresses out of a chifferobe. "Y'all saw it. There's one big room and a good-sized kitchen downstairs. Then the attic will probably need at least one bed in case they have company overnight."

"Everything seems to have something in it," Celia observed. "Are we supposed to unload whatever we're giving them? And where do we put the stuff?" she asked, looking around the crowded attic.

"Now that's a good question," Mandie said, glancing about. "Why don't we just open and shut everything as we go, and see what we can find that is empty? We can't just throw everything out onto the floor. We'll have to find some empty furniture to put it in."

Hilda silently joined the others as they moved about looking for empty drawers, trunks, or wardrobes, but she constantly held her hand over her apron pocket, protecting the object she had dug out of the mine.

All the furniture they went through was crammed full of clothes or other things, until the girls got to the far corner of the attic. Then they opened drawer after drawer and door after door and found them all empty.

"That's funny," Mandie remarked. "Everything is full and running over except right here, and there's not even a string or a hairpin in the furniture in this corner."

"Maybe this is the last stuff put up here and someone emptied it all out," Celia suggested, surveying the jumble of chairs, beds, chifferobes, tables, and trunks.

"I do not think so," Sallie said. "This corner is the farthest from the door. I think it would be the first to be filled up."

"You're right, Sallie," Mandie agreed, turning around. "Look at the pile between here and the door. It would have been impossible to bring this stuff over here through all that mess."

"Then I wonder why all this furniture is empty," Celia said.

"Maybe Uncle John knows. We can ask him. Anyway, if all this furniture is the oldest, it is probably the most valuable, so we might as well pick out something else," Mandie said, going over to a huge wardrobe near the window.

Celia and Sallie followed her. Hilda stayed among the empty furniture, opening and closing drawers as she hummed to herself.

When Mandie opened the wardrobe, to everyone's surprise, there were dolls, dolls, and more dolls—of all sizes, and dressed in various costumes.

"Look!" Mandie cried, reaching for one of them. It was a beautiful doll with a porcelain head, arms, hands, and feet, dressed in white silk, embroidered with blue. "How beautiful!"

The other two girls each took a doll from the wardrobe. Celia got a boy clown—all red, white, and blue. Sallie caressed a beautiful blonde doll dressed in blue organdy.

Hilda, who was watching them from a distance, came running to the wardrobe and quickly seized a doll for herself. She chose a tall, dark-haired bride with a flowing veil, and hugged the doll to herself, humming.

"Where do you suppose all these dolls came from?" Celia gasped. "I never saw so many in my life."

"And they are all so beautiful!" Sallie added.

"We'll certainly have to ask Uncle John about these," Mandie told the girls. "Let's keep out the ones we have and take them downstairs when we go."

"Do you think it will be all right?" Sallie asked, still admiring the doll she held.

"I don't see what harm it could do to take them downstairs," Mandie replied. Then, although she didn't hear anything, she suddenly sensed someone behind them. She turned to see Uncle Ned standing in the doorway of the attic. "Come in, Uncle Ned, and see all these beautiful dolls we found."

Uncle Ned rushed to the wardrobe. "Put back! Put back!" he ordered.

The girls looked at him in astonishment and just stood there with the dolls in their arms.

The old Indian reached for the doll Mandie was holding. Reluctantly, Mandie handed it to him. "But, Uncle Ned, we aren't hurting them," she said. "Who put them in here, anyway? Where did they come from?"

Uncle Ned silently took the dolls from Celia and Sallie and quickly replaced them in the wardrobe. Hilda turned and ran down the stairs with the one she was holding.

"Get doll!" Uncle Ned shouted as Hilda disappeared down the stairway.

Mandie raised her eyebrows and hurried after Hilda, catching her in the hall. It was all she could do to pry the doll away from her. When Mandie finally got it free and started back up the stairs with it, Hilda stomped her feet and screamed. Mandie ignored her and hurried to give Uncle Ned the doll.

"Must not open again," Uncle Ned told the puzzled girls as he closed the doors of the wardrobe.

"But why, Uncle Ned? Who owns all these?" Mandie asked.

"It's a shame to shut all those beautiful dolls in that old wardrobe," Celia said.

Sallie watched her grandfather silently for a while. Finally she spoke. "My grandfather, you know something about these dolls. Please tell us why they are so special."

"My granddaughter, that is not for you to know," the old Indian replied.

"Uncle Ned, you have become so secretive about everything lately," Mandie said. "I share my secrets with you. Please won't you share yours with me?"

Uncle Ned put an arm around Mandie's shoulders. "Papoose, everything not for telling," he said. "Some things must be secret."

"But why, Uncle Ned? Why can't you tell us about these dolls?" Mandie insisted.

"I made promise," Uncle Ned replied.

"Promise? You promised who?" Mandie asked.

"It happen long ago, Papoose. Sad story," the old Indian told her. Then, making sure the doors of the wardrobe were closed tightly, he spoke to all the girls. "No lock. You promise not to open?"

They nodded.

"I will ask Uncle John about the dolls, Uncle Ned," Mandie said.

"John Shaw say it time to look for Snowball. I come get you," the Indian said.

"Oh, let's go," Mandie said, quickly leading the way down the stairs, removing her scarf from her hair as she went. "Wait for us, Uncle Ned. We've got to get our bonnets."

But as the girls ran to Mandie's room and put on their shawls and bonnets, they completely forgot about Hilda.

Outside, Jason Bond had the girls' ponies waiting alongside Uncle Ned's horse.

Mandie and Joe had told Uncle Ned where they had been washed onto the bank, and Uncle Ned led the way.

"Where are Joe and Dimar?" Mandie asked as she rode alongside the old Indian.

"Still at farmhouse. Will go to mine after meal. We hurry. Must be back to eat," Uncle Ned told her.

When they arrived at the place on the riverbank where Snowball had disappeared, Mandie explained again what had happened. "He jumped out of the boat when it hit that old limb out there. And he ran straight into the bushes. We know he didn't get lost in the river."

"We walk," Uncle Ned told the girls as they all dismounted. He tied the animals to a nearby tree. "We call. We look," he said. "We stay together. Do not get out of sight."

Mandie stooped low to peer into the bushes as she went. "Snowball! Snowball!" she called. "Here, kitty, kitty."

"Pretty kitty," Sallie joined in.

"Where are you, Snowball?" Celia called.

Uncle Ned walked along, tapping the bushes with a long stick to shoo the kitten out if he was hiding.

Sallie looked carefully for paw prints along the water's edge.

Mandie called to her. "You're wasting your time, Sallie. He didn't walk along the bank. He landed on that old dead limb out there in the water, and he leaped from the limb onto dry land."

"Then I will look on dry land," Sallie said, coming back inland to continue looking.

"Kittens don't make tracks in dry dirt, do they?" Celia asked.

"Yes, sometimes there is an impression in loose, dry soil," Sallie replied.

After what seemed like hours of back-breaking bending and stooping, Uncle Ned called an end to the search. "Snowball not here," he told the girls. "We go back."

Tears filled Mandie's blue eyes as she realized the impact of those words.

"But, Uncle Ned, he was here," Mandie argued.

"Gone somewhere else," Uncle Ned declared. "Come." He started toward his horse, and the girls followed.

Mandie slowly brought up the rear. "Uncle Ned, can't I stay here awhile? He might come back," she begged.

"John Shaw say no one out of my sight." Uncle Ned turned to look at Mandie. Seeing the tears streaming down her cheeks, he bent to put his arm around her. "Do not cry, Papoose," he said. "I will ask Cherokees to find lost kitten."

Mandie brightened. "Oh, will you, Uncle Ned? I know the Cherokees can find him."

"We see. Now we go," the old Indian said, helping the girls onto their ponies.

When they arrived back at John Shaw's house, the other men and the boys were already there, and it was time for the noon meal.

Everyone was in the parlor except John. They all looked at Mandie when she and the girls entered the room. They knew without a word that the search for the kitten had been unsuccessful.

Joe stepped forward and took Mandie's hand. "Don't give up. We'll look again," he promised her.

"He'll starve to death if we don't find him soon," Mandie said with a catch in her voice.

Just then Mandie heard someone hurrying down the stairs outside the doorway. Uncle John stopped at the door of the parlor and frowned. "Where in the world did all those dolls come from?" he asked. "They're all over the steps from the third floor going up to the attic."

The girls looked at each other in surprise.

"All over the steps, Uncle John?" Mandie inquired.

"Yes, there must be dozens of them. Whom do they belong to?" he asked.

Sallie looked again at Mandie. "Where's Hilda?"

"Why, I thought Hilda was with you girls," said Elizabeth from the settee. "I hope to goodness she's not wandered off somewhere again."

Elizabeth got up and started toward the stairs, but Mandie stopped her. "Never mind, Mother," she said. "We'll go find her. She's upstairs somewhere."

Celia gasped. "Hilda put all those dolls on the steps because you took that one away from her!"

Uncle Ned looked upset as he listened to the conversation. "Dolls must go back," he stated, looking at John.

"Go back? Where? Uncle Ned, what do you know about those dolls?" John asked.

"I promise long ago," Uncle Ned replied. "Must keep promise."

"Promised what?" John asked.

"I promise keep dolls safe," the old Indian finally answered.

"Then you do know something about these dolls. Where did they come from?" Uncle John asked.

The old Indian hesitated, looking around. "We talk. Private," he said, turning to lead the way out of the room.

Mandie rushed over to him, placing a restraining hand on his arm. "Uncle Ned, may I go, too? Please," she begged.

Uncle Ned thought for a moment. "Yes, you and John Shaw," he replied.

Mandie and John followed the old Indian into the sunroom down the hallway. Sitting down, they waited for Uncle Ned to speak.

"Long ago, father of John Shaw marry Talitha Pindar

in this house," Uncle Ned began, not seeming to know how to start. "Much love."

Mandie and her uncle silently waited.

"Have papooses, John and Jim," the Indian continued.

"We know all this, Uncle Ned," John reminded him.

"But John Shaw not know they have girl papoose," Uncle Ned replied.

"A girl?" John asked quickly.

"My father had a sister?" Mandie could hardly believe it.

"Name Ruby, for rubies in mine," Uncle Ned continued. "Born 1840, eight years before John come."

"Where is she? What happened to her? Why didn't anyone ever tell me about her?" John was full of questions.

"Big God come down and take her home. Accident when Ruby ten years old. John Shaw two years old, not remember her," Uncle Ned explained.

John drew a deep breath. "I don't understand why no one ever told me about her."

"Father and mother of John Shaw broken hearts. Not talk about Ruby," Uncle Ned explained.

"So no one else talked about it, either," John said. "What kind of an accident was it, Uncle Ned? How did she die?"

"Bad accident," the old Indian replied. "Fall off pony. Break neck."

Mandie flinched. "Then all the dolls in the wardrobe belonged to Ruby, didn't they?"

"Yes, I promise mother and father of John Shaw I take care of dolls always," the old Indian said sadly.

Mandie explained to Uncle John how they had found

the dolls in the wardrobe in the attic that morning. "And it was probably Hilda who put them all over the stairs," she added.

"Must be." Uncle Ned nodded his head.

"Where is Ruby buried, Uncle Ned?" John asked. "I don't remember ever seeing a grave with that name on it in the family cemetery across the street."

"Ruby there. Stone damaged by Yankee soldiers in war," Uncle Ned explained. "I show John Shaw where."

"After we eat, let's walk over there for a minute, Uncle Ned, and you show me where the grave is," John said.

"May I come, too?" Mandie asked.

"Why, yes, Amanda, but I'd say we shouldn't discuss this in front of the others until after we go over there," Uncle John said. "Now run and see if you can find Hilda so we can eat."

Mandie found Hilda in the attic, sitting on the floor, surrounded by dolls, and carefully examining each one.

"Come on, Hilda. It's time to eat," Mandie told the girl.

Hilda shied away from Mandie, clutching a doll in her arms and holding her other hand over her apron pocket. "No!" the girl refused.

Mandie reached for her hand. "Yes!" she insisted. "It's all right. You can hold that doll, but we have to put all the others back as soon as we eat. Now we'll go by my room, and you can put that doll on the bed so it can sleep until we come back."

Hilda just sat there silently.

"You don't have to keep holding your pocket. I'm not going to take whatever you found at the mine," Mandie assured her. "Now come on. Let's go."

Hilda reluctantly agreed, bringing the bride doll with her.

As they stopped by Mandie's room, she coaxed Hilda to leave the doll on the bed. Hilda carefully covered it with a shawl, humming to it.

At the noon meal, the conversation centered around Jake and Ludie Burns. They looked extremely happy, as if they couldn't believe everything that was happening to them.

"We went through the furniture in the attic this morning, Mrs. Burns," said Mandie. "As soon as Uncle John looks it over, we'll start taking it over to your house."

"The paint won't be dry enough until tomorrow," Dr. Woodard reminded her.

"Besides, we're going mining this afternoon, remember?" Celia remarked.

Elizabeth looked at Mandie sternly. "Not unless an adult goes along and stays with you all every minute," she said.

"That's a good idea," Mrs. Woodard said.

Mandie glanced around the table. "Well, who is going with us?"

"If you young people are going to the mine, then we men will go finish Jake and Ludie's house," Uncle John said.

Mandie looked over at Uncle Ned but didn't say anything.

The old Indian smiled at her. "I will go with Papoose. I watch over Papoose and friends."

"Thank you, Uncle Ned," Mandie said, smiling back at him.

"Thank you, my grandfather," Sallie echoed.

"Before y'all rush off to the mine," John said, rising. "Mandie and I have an errand with Uncle Ned. It won't take more than fifteen minutes. Y'all just stay here at the table and eat. We'll be right back."

A slight frown creased Elizabeth's forehead. "Where are you going?"

"I'll explain later, dear. It's important," John told her. He bent to kiss her cheek as he headed outside with Uncle Ned and Mandie.

The three crossed the road in front of the house and entered the walled-in cemetery behind the church. Uncle Ned led the way, walking directly to a monument with an angel on top of it. The inscription was cracked and illegible. There was a huge piece of the stone missing. Mandie and John stooped down to look closer.

"All I can make out is 1850," John informed them, squinting at the broken marble.

"Ruby die 1850," Uncle Ned said.

"There!" Mandie exclaimed, pointing to one line. "That says *Ruby*, but the *b* is missing."

John looked closer. "It certainly does, and I believe the next part says *Beloved Daughter*, although some of those letters are missing, too."

"Uncle John, there is the name *Shaw* right beneath the angel," Mandie told him. "It's all cracked, but I'm sure it is Shaw."

"I believe you're right, Amanda," John said, standing up. "Uncle Ned, do you remember which stone mason put this monument up? He might have a copy of the inscription. We could have a new marker made."

"Words on paper in wardrobe with dolls," Uncle Ned told him. "Tom Gentry put up stone. Die many years ago."

"I know where the wardrobe is in the attic, Uncle John," Mandie said. "Come on. I'll show you."

The three of them went up to the attic while the others

were still waiting in the dining room.

Stepping between the dolls on the stairs, Uncle John said, "Amanda, you'll get these dolls off the steps, won't you? Someone could trip on them."

"I will, Uncle John," Mandie said, hurrying ahead. "Here's the wardrobe." She opened it for her uncle. "Where's the paper, Uncle Ned?"

The Indian stepped forward and pulled out the big drawer across the bottom. It was filled with papers. He picked up a large brown envelope and handed it to John.

John Shaw sat down in an old rocker behind him and pulled out the contents of the envelope. Mandie leaned over his shoulder.

"My goodness, here's my mother and father's marriage license! I've never seen that before!" John exclaimed, holding up a paper with a seal on it for Mandie to see. "And here is Ruby's baptismal certificate. Let's see. Ruby May Shaw, born May 6, 1840, in this house. Parents—John Shaw, Sr., and Talitha Pindar Shaw. Now, let's see what else is here."

Mandie was reading over his shoulder, itching to get her hands on the papers. "There it is, Uncle John. That paper right there has the name *Tom Gentry* on it," Mandie said, pointing.

John opened the half-folded paper and found the inscription as given to Tom Gentry by John's father. He read from it. " 'An angel Sent to John and Talitha Shaw on May 6, 1840, and Returned to God on May 1, 1850. Ruby May, Beloved Daughter. We Will Meet You In The Morning.' " Uncle John's voice quivered a little at the end, and he took a deep breath.

Mandie wiped a tear from her eye. "How sad," she whispered.

"Yes, and to think no one ever told me I had a sister," John said. He looked up at Uncle Ned. "Who else was here when this happened besides you and Morning Star? Was Aunt Lou here?"

"No. She come after," Uncle Ned replied. "Just Morning Star and me. All others dead now."

Uncle John seemed puzzled. "I'm trying to figure out some dates," he said. "I was two when she died. Jim wasn't born until I was almost fifteen, and my mother died when Jim was a few months old. But my father didn't die until about five years after that. I don't understand why he never told me about my sister."

"Broke his heart. Not talk to anybody about Ruby. Not allowed to say her name," Uncle Ned stated.

John Shaw placed the papers back inside the envelope, stood up, and dropped the envelope inside the open drawer. "Right now we have to get back to the dining room. I'll go through those papers later," he said.

"Are we going to put up a new monument for Ruby?" Mandie asked.

"I'd much rather recut or repair the original stone because my father put it there, but if that can't be done, then we'll get a new one," Uncle John decided. "The War Between the States was over three years before he died. I don't see why he didn't replace it or have it repaired. He certainly had the money to do it."

"Refused to go to cemetery. Never went to look at grave. Not know it broken. He say, 'My Ruby not dead. She well and happy with Big God,' " Uncle Ned told them.

"Well, let's go," Uncle John said, leading the way. "Amanda, can you get the girls to help you put those dolls back in the wardrobe before you go to the mine?"

"I'm sure they'll help," Mandie replied. "It won't take

but a couple of minutes because everyone is anxious to dig for rubies."

John put his hand on Uncle Ned's shoulder. "Please don't let these young people out of your sight for one minute," he cautioned. "You know how fast Amanda can get into trouble."

Mandie looked up at her uncle. "I promise to be real good this time," she said. "And Uncle Ned will be there to make sure I am."

Uncle Ned grunted. "Papoose will keep promise this time. I see to that."

Chapter 12 / The Secret of the Mine

Since there were six young people going to the mine, Uncle Ned took them in his wagon.

"I keep all together better," he explained as they piled in for the ride.

"And this way we'll have something to bring back all those rubies in that we're going to find," Joe joked.

"So far, Hilda is the only one who has found anything. And she won't take it out of her apron pocket, whatever it is," Mandie said, glancing over at her.

Hilda immediately put her hand over her pocket and smiled at Mandie.

"I don't think that would be considered finding anything," Celia concluded, "if it was just a piece of broken pottery."

"But she is proud of it," Dimar added. "And she is afraid we will take it away from her, so she keeps it hidden."

"She does not know all of us well," Sallie said.

Uncle Ned drew up near the entrance to the mine. "Go. Dig," he told them. "I wait here. Watch." He waved them on.

The boys lighted the lanterns, and the young people quickly scrambled down from the wagon to race for the entrance.

Inside, they grabbed tools and began to work. Joe pumped the water to get it going into the trough.

Hilda picked up a hoe and went over to a corner by herself. She began to dig in one spot.

"I'm glad we got all the work done that we could do, so we didn't have to go back to the farmhouse with the men," Joe remarked.

"It is nice to get a chance to dig for rubies," Dimar agreed. "Especially with so many pretty girls," he added with a twinkle in his eye.

"I'm glad you fellas could come with us. There's no telling what we might need you for," Mandie teased. "And Jake Burns is going to take over this mine soon, so we need to dig all we can."

Celia straightened up from her digging for a moment. "Your uncle is being awfully nice to them after what they did to you and Joe," she remarked.

"Uncle John believes that we should return good for evil," Mandie said. "And so do I. We also believe that Mr. and Mrs. Burns are truly sorry for what they did. Uncle John and I talked about it."

"Is that why he took you out of the dining room with him this morning?" Celia asked.

"No," Mandie said, leaning on her hoe. "It seems that my father and Uncle John had a sister a long time ago that they didn't know about."

Everyone stopped to listen as Mandie told them the story of Ruby May.

"And you say she had an accident on her pony and was killed?" Joe said. "I wonder where that happened."

"I didn't even think to ask Uncle Ned about that. You see, he and Morning Star were living with Uncle John and his family when it happened," Mandie explained.

"I told you my grandfather could keep a secret," Sallie said.

"Oh!" Mandie said excitedly. "I forgot to tell you something about Ruby May. All those dolls on the stairs belonged to her. Can you imagine one girl owning that many dolls?"

"Well, if you're rich—and you like dolls," Joe surmised. "Where'd the dolls come from?"

Mandie explained to the boys about the wardrobe in the attic.

"I'm glad you don't still play with dolls," Joe said.

"Me? Why?" Mandie asked.

"Because that is a waste of time," Joe replied. "There are so many other things that a girl should learn about—boys, too, for that matter—before they grow up," Joe replied.

"Such as what? Mandie asked.

"Such as—"

Suddenly there was a loud scream from Hilda in the corner. She stood still, staring at a place where she had been digging.

The others rushed over to her. At first everyone stared silently at the dirt. Then Celia screamed, and Sallie backed off.

"What is it?" Mandie gasped, bending to inspect.

"Do not touch it!" Dimar warned. "Now we know. This is an Indian burial ground we are digging in!"

Uncle Ned, having heard the screams, came to see what it was all about.

When Mandie saw him, she called to him. "Uncle Ned,

come see what Hilda has dug up."

The old Indian walked quickly to the spot. Without inspecting the ground, he said sadly, "I know. It is the burying ground of my ancestors."

Tears moistened Mandie's eyes. "Oh, Uncle Ned, we're sorry. We didn't know."

"Someone should have told us," Joe added.

"I knew there was something funny about this place, the way you and Mrs. Taft and that Jake Burns have been acting," Celia said to Uncle Ned. "They knew all the time, didn't they?"

Uncle Ned nodded. "Cherokee tradition say you dig here, you disturb spirits of ancestors. In past, we worship Cherokee ancestors. We Christians now. Know this wrong. Worship only Big God. But must respect burying ground."

Dimar stepped forward. "We will cover it back up," he told him, picking up his hoe.

"Cover what up?" Uncle John asked as he came down the steps with Dr. Woodard and Jake Burns.

"Uncle John, we've uncovered an Indian burial ground," Mandie explained, tears glistening in her eyes.

John Shaw and Dr. Woodard stepped forward to look while Jake Burns stayed in the background. Turning to Jake, John asked, "Do you know anything about this?"

Jake stuttered as he answered. "A l-l-little."

"Well, what do you know about it?" John asked firmly.

"That is the reason this mine was closed," Jake admitted, hanging his head. "Uncle Ned knew about that. But only that part of the mine over there is a burial ground. If you turn back this way, it's all clear."

John shook his head slowly. "Now, Uncle Ned, I see why you called this a sad, bad mine," he said. Then he looked back at Jake. "When you agreed to work it for us, were you planning to dig right through the graves under here?"

"Why, no," Jake said. "Like I said, I knew about the burial ground. I was plannin' to expand in the other direction. I wasn't goin' to disturb the graves over that way."

"I'm sorry, Uncle Ned," John said. "If you had only spoken up and let us know about this, we never would have opened this mine again."

"White man not understand Cherokee ways," Uncle Ned replied.

Mandie took hold of her old Indian friend's hand. "But, Uncle Ned, we're part Cherokee," she said. "We would have understood."

Jake stepped forward hesitantly. "That's not the only reason this here mine was closed up," he said.

"What do you mean by that?" Dr. Woodard asked.

"My pa was killed here after he closed the mine. Nobody could ever figure out how or who did it, but the Cherokees claimed it was their ancestors takin' revenge on the white men who disturbed their spirits."

"Did my father believe that?" John asked.

"Your pa didn't, but your ma did. Remember, she was full-blooded Cherokee," Jake reminded him.

John Shaw turned to look at Uncle Ned.

The old Indian finally spoke up. "Cherokees have many superstitions about mine," he acknowledged. "Ruby come here. She ride pony. Pony go wild and throw her. Your father close mine. Say it never be opened again."

"I wish somebody had told me about all this," John sighed. "I wouldn't have opened the mine for anything."

"I not tell you what do, John Shaw. Your mine," Uncle Ned told him.

"That's right, John. It's yours to do what you like," Jake said.

"Uncle John, couldn't we go on with what Mr. Burns was planning?" Mandie asked. "We could put a wall around this side and close it off, and then work in the other direction."

"Would that be agreeable to you, Uncle Ned?" John asked. "I don't want to do anything to hurt you. These are your ancestors buried here, and this place is as sacred as our own family cemetery."

Uncle Ned thought for a moment. All the young people silently waited for his answer.

"Agree. Do not disturb graves of ancestors," the old Indian murmured faintly.

"Thanks, Uncle Ned." Mandie squeezed his hand hard.

Everyone breathed a sigh of relief.

"All right, Jake, you heard the agreement," John said. "This area is to be walled off and not disturbed."

"Yes, sir," Jake replied. "We'll find more rubies in the other direction anyway."

Hilda, who had been crouching in a corner away from the others, walked slowly toward them. Putting her hand in her pocket, Hilda took out the object she had been hiding and handed it to Mandie.

The other young people quickly crowded around to see what it was.

Mandie looked in her hand, then shivered and tossed the object to Joe.

He caught it in midair. "Oh, no!" he cried.

"What is it?" Celia asked.

Joe examined it more closely. "I think it is part of one of Uncle Ned's ancestors," he said.

The other young people stepped back. Joe handed the small bone to the old Indian, who inspected it closely. Walking over to the opening where Hilda had dug, Uncle Ned knelt down and laid the bone in the ground with the other pieces of the skeleton. Reaching for the hoe, he silently pushed the loose dirt back over the opening.

Sallie and Dimar knelt by Uncle Ned beside the freshly covered grave. Then as the old Indian raised his voice in Cherokee prayer, they all fell silent and bowed their heads.

When the Indians rose, Hilda stepped toward them and said, "Rest in peace."

Everyone looked at her in amazement.

"How did Hilda know what they were saying?" Joe asked. "Does Hilda speak Cherokee?"

Dr. Woodard cleared his throat. "I'm beginning to wonder if Hilda is part Cherokee," he speculated.

"Dimar said he was teaching her the Cherokee language," Mandie told him.

"But I have not been able to teach her much," Dimar stated. "I did not teach her those words."

Hilda looked over at Dimar and smiled. "Cher'kee," she said softly.

"You know, John, maybe that's our trouble with Hilda. She may not understand English," Dr. Woodard said.

"But you said you met her parents. They weren't Cherokee, were they?" John asked.

"They spoke English, but they did look like they could have been Indian, come to think of it," Dr. Woodard concluded. "I'll have to check that out."

"I think we should all call it a day and go home now," Uncle John decided.

The young people groaned in disappointment.

"Could I get just one more sieveful?" Joe asked. "Please?"

"All right, just one more sieve each, and then we'll go," Uncle John agreed.

The young people rushed to fill their sieves and then hurried to the water trough. But again they each groaned as they emptied the gravel—all except Joe.

Joe suddenly called to John as he held his sieve over the water. "Mr. Shaw, please come and see what I have here."

John picked up the object Joe had in the sieve, turned it over and over, and held it next to the lantern. "Looks like you've got a good-sized ruby there," he stated, handing the stone back to him.

"A real ruby?" Joe exclaimed.

"An honest-to-goodness ruby, Joe," John answered.

There was so much excitement among the young people that Uncle John finally allowed one more sieve each, but no one came up with anything but gravel and rocks.

As the group climbed back into Uncle Ned's wagon, Mandie sat next to Joe. "What are you going to do with your ruby, Joe?" she asked.

"I guess I'll get it cut and polished like you're supposed to do," he replied, turning the stone over and over in his hand. "I can't believe I found a real ruby!"

"After you get it cut and polished, what are you going to do with it?" Celia wanted to know.

"I'll—uh—I'll just—I'll just keep it," Joe said, glancing at Mandie.

But Mandie wasn't listening anymore. She was thinking of her lost kitten. She couldn't wait to get home to
find out if he had come back.

When they all got back to the house, Liza let them in.

"Liza, has Snowball come home?" Mandie asked immediately.

"Missy, I ain't seed hide nor hair of dat white cat," Liza
told her.

"I'm afraid he's lost and can't find the way home,"
Mandie said. "Just in case you happen to see him, will
you let me know right that minute?"

"I sho' will, Missy," Liza said sympathetically. "Supper
bein' put on de table. Hurry now."

After they all cleaned up and gathered at the dining
table for the evening meal, the young people excitedly
told the women about what had happened at the mine.
The ladies were horrified at the thought of digging up
graves.

"John, you're not going to let people go in there and
dig now that we know about the burial ground, are you?"
Elizabeth asked.

"No, of course not, Elizabeth," John replied. "We're
closing off that part."

"May we go back and dig in the other part again
before we go back to school?" Mandie asked.

"If you have time," Uncle John said. "Tomorrow is
Thanksgiving. Morning Star will be here in the morning.
We thought if everybody got together then, we could get
all the furniture moved into Jake and Ludie's house while
the dinner is cooking. It would be a nice Thanksgiving
gesture."

Everyone approved the plan, and bright and early the
next morning, Morning Star arrived and they gathered in

the attic. Piece by piece, Uncle John approved the furniture that they were taking to the Burns's house.

Ludie, standing nearby, gasped when she saw what she was being given. "Mr. Shaw," she said, "we couldn't possibly take all that nice furniture. It cost too much."

"Ludie, don't worry about it. You and Jake will be working for it. Besides, I don't know that we'll ever need it. No sense in letting it sit here and rot," John argued.

The men pushed a huge sideboard forward to take downstairs.

As Mandie and the other girls stepped back, Mandie spied a paper tacked to the back of the sideboard. She ran forward to get a closer look. "Stop!" she yelled excitedly. "Wait! I've found something!"

Joe, standing nearby, quickly looked to see what it was. "Looks like a map to some hidden treasure," he said.

"Treasure?" the young people echoed.

"What's this all about?" John Shaw asked, stooping behind the sideboard. He looked closely at the large piece of old crumbling paper tacked there, then carefully pulled out the tacks holding it. He straightened up with the drawing in his hands. "This has my sister Ruby's name on it," he said, laying it down on top of the sideboard.

Everyone crowded around to look.

The drawing, dimmed by time, was labeled: My House, River, Rose Creek, Ruby Mine, Your House, Rhododendron Bush, Persimmon Tree, Rockpile, and the Path to Hezekiah's House.

"Look! It has directions, too!" Mandie exclaimed, pointing to the printing at the bottom. She read aloud. " 'Go down the path to Hezekiah's House. Turn left and go 936 feet to Rockpile. Go right 572 feet to Persimmon Tree. Then go left 333 feet to Rhododendron Bush. Dig three feet under Rhododendron Bush. That is where Treasure is buried.' " Mandie looked up. "I wonder where all this is," she said.

"The *My House* would have to be this house if Ruby drew it," Celia reasoned.

"And there is the ruby mine," Sallie pointed.

"But who is Hezekiah?" Dimar asked.

"Do you know who Hezekiah is, Uncle John?" Mandie asked.

"I don't remember ever knowing anyone by that name. But then if you will notice, this map was drawn April 30, 1850," John replied. "I was only two years old then."

"That was the day before she died. What a coincidence," Mandie said in wonderment.

"It certainly was," Uncle John agreed. He turned to Jake. "Did you ever know anyone around here name Hezekiah?"

"No, John. Don't believe I do," Jake replied. "You see, when I was growing up, we lived in an old house right across the river from the mine. I wasn't allowed to go anywhere but to the mine and back. Then, too, we wouldn't have had the same friends as your family."

Dimar leaned forward. "The place called *Your House* on this map looks like it might be the old farmhouse we are fixing up for Mr. and Mrs. Burns," he said.

"Yeah, it might be," Jake agreed.

"I wonder what the treasure was?" Ludie said.

"Was? I hope it still *is* because I am going to find it," Mandie declared. "Who wants to go with me?"

"You are not going anywhere, young lady—not until we finish moving these things for Mr. and Mrs. Burns. And by that time the Thanksgiving turkey will be done," Uncle

John said. "Now let's get back to work here."

"May I take the map, Uncle John?" Mandie asked.

"I think we'd better put it in that drawer with the other papers over there until we get time to look into it," Uncle John replied. "It might be valuable." He winked at her and smiled.

Reluctantly, Mandie crossed the room to the old wardrobe with the dolls and carefully added the map to the papers in the drawer.

The treasure map was the topic of conversation all morning. The girls helped as much as they could, taking turns going downstairs to open the front door for the men carrrying the heavy furniture.

As Uncle Ned was tugging a huge chair through the attic doorway, Mandie came to help.

"I'll open the front door for you, Uncle Ned," she offered, walking ahead of him down the three flights of steps.

In the front hallway, she paused with her hand on the doorknob as Uncle Ned set the chair down for a minute to get his breath. "I think you should have had some help bringing that thing down the stairs," she said.

"Not heavy. Open door now," the old Indian told her.

Mandie flung the door wide and stared out onto the porch in disbelief. There, huddled on the doormat, sat Snowball, meowing weakly.

"Snowball!" Mandie cried as the kitten limped toward her. "Oh, your foot is hurt!" She picked him up and hugged him tightly.

Suddenly his disheveled, dirty body went limp.

Mandie panicked. "Dear God," she prayed, "please don't let Snowball die." Tears trickled down her cheeks as she sat down in the middle of the porch, holding the kitten. Uncle Ned bent over her to look.

The white kitten's dirty fur was covered with briars. Uncle Ned rubbed his hand across the kitten's face. The kitten didn't move. "Do not hold too tight," he said. "Snowball weak, not eat."

Mandie loosened her hold on the kitten and held him up to her face. "Please don't let him die, dear God, please!" she cried again.

At that moment Snowball perked up and lifted his head, then meowed and snuggled against her shoulder.

Mandie was so happy that it was all she could do to keep from squeezing the kitten to death. "Thank you, dear God! Thank you!" she cried.

Uncle Ned sat down on the porch beside her and took her hand in his. "Papoose see what trouble disobedience cause," the old man said. "Must learn to obey. Keep promises."

"You're right, Uncle Ned," Mandie admitted, squeezing his hand. "Let's thank God for sending Snowball home."

The two sat there and looked toward the sky.

"Dear God," Mandie began with tears in her eyes. "Thank you for sending Snowball home. I love him so much. Thank you again for forgiving me for causing trouble. Help me to think before I do things. Thank you, dear God."

"Thank you, Big God," Uncle Ned added.

Mandie cuddled the kitten as she stood up. "I've got to get Snowball something to eat and see what's wrong with his little paw," she said.

"Me see paw," Uncle Ned stated, rising. He examined the kitten. "Here. Thorn in paw. We get out. Hold."

Mandie held the hurt little paw while Uncle Ned

worked on it. Snowball meowed weakly and tried to pull his paw away, but Uncle Ned held it firm and pulled out the thorn.

"Must get medicine now," the Indian told her.

"Thank you, Uncle Ned," Mandie said. "I'll go bathe it and put some medicine on it."

"Papoose not going to look for treasure?" he asked.

Mandie grinned at him. "Not yet, Uncle Ned. You see, I stopped to think first. I'll go when Uncle John gives me permission. Right now I'll go doctor Snowball."

"Good girl." Uncle Ned smiled back. "Ruby good girl, too. I hope you find Ruby's treasure."

"I will," Mandie promised. "All in good time."